Adventure *in* ANCIENT AZORKA

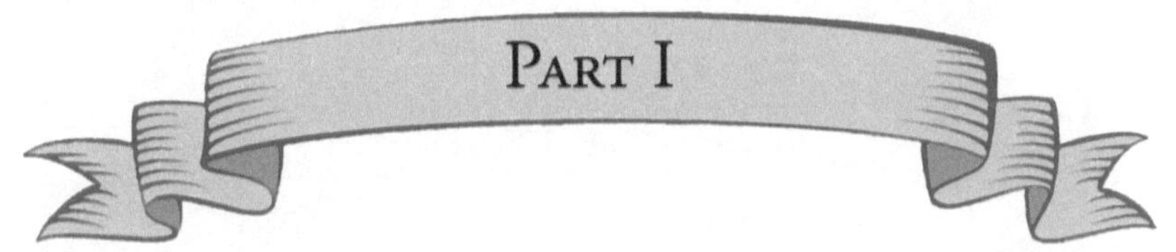

CORRIE GILMOUR

BLUEPRINT PRESS
INTERNATIONALE

ISBN
978-1-961117-51-8(Paperback)
978-1-961117-52-5(eBook)
978-1-961117-50-1(Hardcover)

Table of Contents

Adventure in Ancient Azorka

Part I

A Page From the Wizard's Day

"Today, two advanced island civilizations hidden in the Atlantic Ocean have opposing solutions for controlling a violent outside world in the year 1688. Our diplomacy has broken down, the stakes are high and the covert war has begun. The Wizard has been experimenting with recombinant DNA and is preparing to attack the world with a horde of intelligent hybrid animal-dragons. Our Guardians' and their flying friends will stop him but the battles will be challenging, some out of this world."

Signed by
Mitch
Guardian for Azorka in the year 1688 AD

FEBRUARY 18, 1688

For years I've known about the centuries old artificial intelligence that hides our two Islands. It keeps us cloaked in a mist or hides our existence through holographic projection. This ancient technology, probably left over from our wars with "Lemuria", activates when selected longitudes and latitudes are crossed over by an invader. I kept this knowledge secret from Azorka. Azorkan sailors were not suspicious of the mist and were not aware of the holographic projections when they appeared for the benefit of approaching ships.

Six years ago I had agreed to a meeting with Azorka's officials and tried to convince them that the population of the Earth had increased enough that discovery was imminent. Eventually the explorers of the outside world would stumble upon us by accident and would become aware of our advanced technology. Hordes of intruders would show up on our shores. We'd be overwhelmed and the "war like" countries would get away with enough fire power to destroy the planet.

My plan called for the organized takeover of the planet using our military technology. We would combine our forces and the world would be scared into submission. Simple demonstrations of our superiority would convince those countries with a lust for war that we would always win in war. The world's governments would surrender and together we would control the successful progress of the planet.

Azorka wouldn't listen to me. I had to make other plans. So now my empire must take action before it's too late. For almost five years the skies of Azorka have been free from the terror of our Queen. Tomorrow that would change!

The sun was sinking into the ocean and dragging a curtain of dark clouds which would obscure the bright sickle moon tonight. Maria relaxed as the stinging rays of the sun would no longer be a discomfort. Traveling north at a leisurely pace she looked around her island. The remaining ambient light revealed mostly rocky hills, some fields and small forests in the distance. The island's most northerly beach faced the enemy island across two hundred miles of ocean.

It was warm for February and Maria thought she heard a chorus of cicadas as she passed over a small forest. Up ahead in the tree tops a dozen crows called up to her then dispersed in terror flying out in all directions when they realized what they had said good evening to. Maria smiled, her green skin shimmered in the faint light as the northern beach came into view. She flew over the beach, its golden sand fading into the cold shadows, and her powerful white wings accelerated to maximum speed, one hundred feet above a calm but icy ocean.

It would take a couple of hours to reach "Azorka" the enemies island home. Maria glanced in a westerly direction and saw a Spanish Armada heading south. The outside world probably sent them to oppose the pirates who had caused death and destruction on popular shipping routes. Presently there were no other ships in the area so Maria rehearsed this evenings mission in her mind dwelling on what may be hidden in the Azorkan bank. If Maria could steal this mighty and deadly source of energy then the balance of power between the two islands would dramatically change.

After another hour Azorka was in sight and soon she was flying over beaches and forests and a mountain that she would stop at on her way home where the specimen for the Wizard could be obtained. Up ahead the forest gave way to a clearing where the main village held the bank. The village was not large and there were very few buildings taller than seventy feet except for two pyramids on the outskirts of town.

Smaller buildings were domed and presently the street lamps gave it all a soft glow. Maria slowed down as she approached the bank. It was a concrete square shaped building with two guards standing side by side at its entrance. They were dressed in dark and tight-fitting clothing designed specially for the military with extra padding to protect the more vulnerable parts of the human body. The guards earned a bow and on their backs was a quiver full of arrows. Maria was certain that the arrows would have copper tips which would cause her great pain. The laser pistols tucked securely in the guards belts would be useless against the force field she was activating now. However, the copper arrows could penetrate the force field so she had to be swift. Hovering in mid air Maria anxiously looked around then rose in the night a little higher so she wouldn't be noticed and planned her attack. She could use her laser gun but it's accuracy was dubious. The Wizard had carefully designed it as a blasting tool intended for the bank's door.

This time brute force would be the solution. Maria's green arms and torso were of human dimension but super-human in strength so she could easily carry her stolen prize back in a metal net now wrapped around her waist. The lower part of her body was reptilian in appearance and very powerful with feet that would be suited to at dragon outfitted with three sharp claws per foot. Maria decided to rely on her super-human strength using her powerful hips, legs and feet to take out the two guards at the same time. She dove swiftly like a fierce bird of prey. In the last instant she pulled up her body and drove her giant feet into the heads of the guards knocking them unconscious and in one fluid movement landing on her feet in front of the bank's thick door. Maria removed the laser gun the Wizard had crafted and depressing the handles built in trigger she let a powerful blast off at the bank's door. Amazingly it held but before she could trigger a second blast a copper arrow grazed her shoulder. Maria tucked the gun into her belt, immediately took flight and as she disappeared into the night she heard them sound the alarm and call out"Dragon Queen!" Below the backup squad that had fired the arrow caught up with the unconscious guards, got them on stretchers and moved them off to the hospital a short distance away.

The commanding officer told his soldiers to spread the news about the Dragon Queen's attack within the military only. Be on the lookout for her and report her on sight. He also arranged for a report of the nights incident to be sent in the morning to the castle for the Royal Family and Guardians of the Kingdom of Azorka. Only one person was left in the dark about the nights events. The military's number one commander General Zen was away on secret business and right now only a guardian could summon him.

CHAPTER 1

The next day a beautiful morning arrived in Azorka. There wasn't a cloud anywhere in a rich blue February sky. The sun warmed the land and filtered down through a cover of old growth forest so thick that the remaining light falling on the school below almost looked like an emerald green. The school was composed of three one level circular buildings with domed roofs made of a durable and clear material which allowed in light and the warmth of the sun. It was the part of the largest village in Azorka which was home to the Kingdom's workers, military, and educators. Jenny was one of those teachers addressing a classroom of fourteen children aged ten years and all experiencing Monday morning lethargy.

"Alright class this morning we're going to review last Friday's lesson. I'm going to need a volunteer to come up to the front and mark down the answers from the questions I ask on the map I've drawn on the board." Jenny said with a smile.

Jenny looked out into the classroom. The children were all dressed in long pants and warm tops in the colors of their choice. Seven students sat expressionless at the first long marble table. The students seated at the second marble table at the back showed a similar lack of enthusiasm except for one girl who quickly put up her hand.

"Wonderfull Susan will help mark down our answers" Jenny said.

Susan was dressed in the same bright yellow sweater that Jenny had selected that morning. But unlike Jenny who had continued with yellow pants tucked into white leather boots, she wore a dark brown pair of pants which were tucked into dark brown leather boots. No one in the classroom wore clothing with artistic patterns like plaid, paisley, or stripes. That was usually saved for special occasions.

As Susan got up out of her seat she pointed up to the roof.

"There's our friend again!" she shouted.

Jenny rolled her eyes as the entire classroom looked up through the roof and into the forest just in time to see a few branches springing up and down halfway up the nearest tree.

"Ok class, settle down! We all know are little friend outside has to wait till recess." Jenny shouted over their voices.

Susan walked up to the blackboard and took up her position beside the map Jenny had drawn for the lesson. Her thick red hair fell to her shoulders and sparkled in the morning light pouring down through the domed roof above. Fortunately, the children were not distracted by the playground outside. The classrooms were arranged in sections within the circular building and the walls were without windows. "Where on the board can we find the Azores Island chain?" Jenny asked.

Tommy in the front row stood up. His hand practically flew out of his dark green sweater. He pointed at the top of the drawing on the blackboard.

"The Azores Island chain is one-hundred miles north of us in the Atlantic Ocean." He said.

"That is correct Tommy. "How long and how wide is Azorka? Do you all remember last week's lesson?" Jenny asked

Another child stood up in the back row. Raj was happy to answer this question as he had been studying hard during the weekend.

"Azorka is an eighty-mile-long Island Kingdom that varies in width from forty miles at its most narrow point in the south and sixty miles wide here in village"B". Raj said.

A slight smile washed over his features because he knew he had given Jenny the right answer.

"You have studied well Raj. Jenny said.

Behind her Susan was writing down his rather long answer as quick as she could. Being the teacher's pet came at a high cost and of course efficiency was expected.

The children's friend outside, also ten years old, was looking down at their classroom from fifty-feet up in a tree. Though the lesson could not be heard outside, the children's friend knew all that was said and was getting an education as well. The children's friend flew over to another tree which branched out over a classroom where a more mature group of students were answering questions from their teacher. Rafick was forty years old but he never tired of teaching the most senior students in the school. He was very popular amongst the student body because he taught sports to students of all ages at the school. Soccer had emerged as the number one favorite.

His ancestors had left Ethiopia five thousand years ago, Immigrating to Azorka and offering knowledge on some of the most advanced health remedies known to mankind at that time.

He ran his hand through his short bushy black hair and asked the students his question.

"Who can tell us some geographical facts about our Kingdom and the Kingdom opposed to us south of here." He said in his deep voice.

Wing put up his hand. He was sixteen and studying to be eligible for Azorka's military school.

"Azorka is well hidden in the Atlantic Ocean. The eighty-mile-long island Kingdom is surrounded by rocks and reef which act as a natural fortification against invading ships. After the war, rock close to the ocean surface was often responsible for sinking ships sailing between the Island Kingdoms. Our area, one-hundred miles south of the Azores Island chain, is usually avoided by sailors and commercial ships."

"It has been many centuries since the war which sent two hundred miles of mainland civilization to the ocean floor and left behind two remaining island Kingdoms, each Kingdom hidden from the outside world. The island Kingdom to the south is home to a population of forty thousand who live underground. Their island is rocky, although there are trees of many different kinds including palm trees on their northern beach. This Kingdom is ruled by a mysterious Wizard and his military commander the Dragon Queen. It has been a constant threat to Azorka and soon the outside world if the Wizard goes unchallenged and completes his evil objectives." Wing finished.

The children's friend knew that Rafick was reviewing last week's lessons. It thought back to Friday. Rafick was in a relaxed mood and he had casually asked the class what the mind set was before the time of war in Azorka. Wolfgang in the back row had answered.

"Governing representatives from the south and north would meet to discuss world affairs. There were arguments concerning the outside world. Were they ready to accept modern technology."

"We had agents in every part of the outside world to monitor the progress of different societies. It was often reported that countries were war like and could put the lives of many at risk if we provided them with our crystal technology. This is technology used to collect and store ultra violet rays from the sun converting and releasing the stored energy under controlled circumstances. This form of energy is used to heat homes, provide lighting and could be used to create tools for industry and geological purposes. Unfortunately, it could also be weaponized."

"The argument for conquering a growing outside world came from the south. This was strictly against Azorka's constitution. We referred to our opposition as rebels. But we didn't expect their betrayal and war against us." Wolfgang had finished.

Wolfgang had sat down and Rafick had thanked him for his detailed answer, then he addressed the class.

"Who can tell me about the'Firestones'. He asked.

Cynthia put up her hand. She was dressed in gold pants and shirt which sparkled from the light filtering through the movement of branches above the glass dome roof. Cynthia had brushed back a lock of fiery red hair as she rose and addressed Rafick and the class.

"Azorka found a deposit of massive blocks of crystallizing quartz and crafted them into an energy source they called a Firestone. The Firestone was installed at the top of a pyramid built over top of the Earth's magnetic ley lines which transferred the energy to a relay station serving the individual needs of the community. After the great flood this was no longer effective and we returned to recharging our crystal. But at the time of this advancement, the rebels turned the Firestone we gave them into a weapon and killed one of our Guardians who had discovered the betrayal. We carried out the same conversion and fired back without knowing that this would cause two-hundred miles of land to sink to the ocean floor. This stopped the war from progressing further." Cynthia finished.

"Thank you, Cynthia, for that excellent answer." Rafick had said.

The recess bell rang and the ten-year-old Zapatsaur, the children's friend, sprang from the branches and flew down to the soccer field. The wings folded tight and neatly to its back and the young Zapatsaur stood upright ready to run after the ball with the other children it anxiously awaited.

Well school was in session, just twenty miles north, the Guardian's castle was barely visible in the old growth forest that made its way up a hill. From a distance it looked like half of an arrows head was sticking upright, sharp end first. From the ocean its grey and white color made it look like a natural rock formation. But when you got close enough it was a megalith that was almost square. The interiors hallway ran for ninety-feet past a massive living room, down to a massive kitchen and at the end of the hallway, a cozy twenty-five foot by twenty-five-foot family room complete with a large fieldstone fireplace and comfortable furniture. It was like a silent sentinel gazing down at village'A' below, where most of Azorka's diplomats and officials lived amongst some of the military's artisans for secret projects.

At the end of the hallway and beyond the large sliding glass doorway, outside on a white marble patio, an anxious Princess was pacing back and forth. She stopped pacing in front of the hand carved wood table and two chairs she had moved into place for her meeting with General Zen. Princess Sally was troubled by a report delivered in the early morning to the castle. It was a report about a lone invader attacking two guards at village'B' and trying to gain entry to the bank by blasting the door with a crudely fashioned, hand held laser tool. The invader was one of Azorka's arch enemies, the Dragon Queen.

Sally was in charge of Azorka while her parents, the King and Queen, were on a covert mission and sailing around the Empire's island in what appeared to be a large fishing vessel. She dreaded the thought of having to deal with Azorka's most frightening adversary. On the other hand, she was getting angry enough that it might become desirable.

The Dragon Queen is a fierce enemy with super human strength. When she was known as Maria, ten-thousand years ago, she had agreed to participate in one of the Wizard's experiments. At the end of the experiment, her skin had turned green from her waist up and her lower half, now twice as large, was covered in green scales ending in large three-digit feet sixteen inches long. The upper half of her body was still human and Maria was still very beautiful with long raven black hair. However, the experiment had granted her two powerful arms which grew out of her back and were attached to powerful white wings, another deformity she would have to live with forever because she was also immortal.

Over the years, Maria trained in the military, and became a brilliant strategist. She learned to use the misshapen hands which attach to the top of her wings with a lethal claw and she used her super-human strength in combat. But she enjoyed her secret missions most of all, probably because she could work alone more successfully.

The two-hundred miles of mainland, that sunk beneath the ocean, was home for many industries dedicated to advanced technologies, and left a wealth of technical information and equipment waiting to be rescued. The Empire and Azorka lost an equal amount of land but before this event, luckily, Azorka had moved most of its laser technology northward.

Princess Sally thought the Dragon Queen was after the gold. This is Azorka's currency for trade with other countries in the outside world, where it sells crafted goods, island fruit and other agricultural products the island is able to grow. Azorka receives gold for its goods and produce and in turn purchases necessary goods for the island. So today the intrepid Princess decided to summon the Army's number one military commander, General Zen for a secret meeting.

It was a beautiful sunny day and Princess Sally dressed in an informal long white robe with baggy white pants, met the General on the patio in the backyard of the castle grounds. Sally was also in charge of the security of Azorka while the King and Queen were absent. Should there be a secret she was not privy to, then Zen would act as advisor. Her sister, Princess Heather, was in charge of Azorka's agricultural produce which is a significant portion of the island Kingdom's source of revenue. As of early this morning young Heather was out tending to her duties, managing Azorka farmland.

The General Zen had arrived from his secret business at the Azorkan research center wearing casual blue pants and a white shirt. He had come immediately as requested, without changing into his uniform.

Zen walked around to the back of the castle and saw Princess Sally gazing out to sea on the patio, looking like she was lost in thought. She was an attractive lady, he thought, which helped to hide her fiery demeanor when she was challenged. Sally turned and smiled pointing to a couple of chairs arranged across from each other at a beautifully hand carved wooden table. While the General took his seat, she thought the athletic thirty-five-year-old General was handsome. His responsibilities were stressful but his dark brown hair crowned a face that was free of wrinkles.

"Thank you for meeting with me General. I know its short notice but it is a serious problem and I need to discuss the implications for Azorka. But before I do, is there anything I can get you?" Sally asked.

"No thanks Sally. I know Indie's got something cooking at home." Zen returned.

"How is Indie doing." Sally asked.

General Zen's wife is a seamstress who teaches her craft at the village school twenty miles south of the castle. She was home early today.

"She's very happy teaching her craft at the school." Zen replied.

"That's good to hear General. I look forward to seeing her latest creation." Sally said.

They both sat down at the table and Zen removed his dark brown cloth hat, placing it on the table. Sally sat across from him and leaning forward, with a serious expression she began to explain the details of last night's attack.

"General, I have summoned you because of a very serious matter. Last night our security team in your village caught the Dragon Queen trying to get into the bank. She sent two of our guards to hospital with serious injuries. She was using a laser gun, obviously one of the Wizard's inventions, on the door of the bank. If our security team hadn't caught her in time she might have succeeded at getting in." Sally finished.

The General was surprised at hearing about this bold attempt and was deeply concerned as he knew of one very valuable item securely locked away in the bank. This was probably what the Dragon Queen was actually attempting to steal. But how would she return it to the Empire's island. It was massive and very heavy.

"She hasn't been seen for five years now. We defeated her last time she was here with our copper arrows. I can still remember her blood curdling scream when my copper arrow penetrated her thigh. Copper won't kill the immortal Dragon Queen but it will cause her intense pain. It's the only substance we know of that is capable of penetrating her invisible shield the Wizard designed for her. Even our laser guns and cannons can't stop her." Zen anxiously explained.

Sally brushed back a lock of her light brown hair and leaned forward in her chair.

"Last night security grazed her shoulder with a copper arrow but she was quick about flying out of range and escaping. I agree it is an effective deterrent. If she'd reacted any slower our team would have pursued her in the night sky on the back of their Zapatsaurs. As it is they don't know what direction she chose to make her escape. Our security teams are out looking for her now, but this attack has been kept secret from the public to avoid panic." Sally explained.

"Would you like me to capture her. We've developed a copper arrow that we believe will cause her to lose consciousness. However, I need to strike her with it while she's on the ground. Otherwise we'd have to deal with injuries from the fall if we hit her in flight. I'd love a chance to see how effective it will be." The General said.

"No General, I would like to see her captured, but this could cause problems for the King and Queen on their mission. If the Dragon Queen doesn't return to her island within a reasonable time, then this may alert the Wizard and interrupt the efforts of the King and Queen." Sally replied.

A look of frustration appeared on Sally's face. The two island Kingdoms have been fighting against each other for centuries. The continuing struggle has been the effort of every generation since the mainland broke up and sunk to the bottom of the ocean.

Azorka was a peaceful Kingdom that kept its existence secret from the outside world. They traded with the outside world secretly by staging goods to be shipped at the largest of the Azores islands, Sao Miguel. Azorka kept a trading post and farmland for five-hundred residents who receive goods from overnight secret shipments of Azorka's produce and crafted goods. Taxes were paid to the government controlling Sao Miguel and no questions were asked.

"I think your right about that, a good decision. We've known for some time that the Wizard is working on something important. We need to find out what. They're not a peaceful Kingdom and looking for ways to conquer the outside world. If the Wizard creates a large enough army of intelligent creatures, he might be successful." The General said.

"They have the precious gems that they mine on their island to trade for other items the outside world might offer. So, we'd have to consider them wealthy enough to achieve their future goals should wealth play a factor in planning their future invasion." Sally reminded.

"They have signed an agreement with us, that guarantees they will not deal with the criminal element. from the outside world; like pirates. But for now, what would you like me to do about the Dragon Queen."

"Presently, I need you to check on the Zapatsaur's mountain home in the morning. I remember five years ago when the Dragon Queen tried to kidnap one of their babies. All of Azorka was in an uproar believing the Wizard wanted to dissect it for his experiments. And for now, I don't want the Dragon Queen captured. If there is an opportunity to observe her movements than please report that to me." Sally said.

The General was sure that the Dragon Queen was after the Firestone which was kept in the bank. This was something only high-ranking military commanders knew about. Sally would learn this and other secrets when she turns twenty-five next year.

"I will do my best and join up with the security teams to check on their progress. I'll check the Zapatsaurs in the morning."The General answered.

He noticed that the wind had picked up while they were talking and looked up at the sky. In the distance dark clouds were heaping up on the horizon and now and then a flash of lightning would light up the growing canopy of clouds.

"Looks like we're in for a storm Sally." He said.

"Yes, it looks that way." She answered.

Sally looked out into the backyard at her own Zapatsaur. They find shelter when it's raining and her Zapatsaur would shelter under the canopy set up in the backyard. The average Zapatsaur was fourteen-feet long from head to tail. They are fully covered with grey scaly segments, of various size, each segment having a small spec of its own color. They have two legs and two arms that are human-like in shape and proportion but much more powerful. Their head and mouth resemble that of a lizard with the exception of wolf-like ears. And two powerful and enormous wings allow it to fly at one-hundred miles per hour. They could also walk upright with their wings neatly folded to their back.

"I do feel special something for the Zapatsaurs. Five thousand years ago we befriended this community of intelligent flying creatures. When we need to go somewhere they are always there for us, thanks to their mental link with the rider. Their children play sports with our children. But we haven't communicated with them as much as we would like to, so I have been working on a pictorial alphabet that just might be a good start in this endeavor. I'll show it to you later."

"Yes, I'd be interested in having a look at that." Zen answered.

The Zapatsaur developed a mental synchronicity with the rider. The rider didn't need to use reins for direction because the Zapatsaur could read the mind of its rider. The rider would hold on to the last of three, half-moon shaped bony segments that ran down its long neck, and kneel comfortably on its back.

Many centuries ago, Azorkans had built their homes, corridors and meeting places in the side of a mountain using laser tools to cut the rock. Each Zapatsaur had their own furnished cave home and were treated like a human being. The Azorkans found they had some of the personal needs of humans so they included a hospital in village'B' for their needs as well. Their village was referred to as village'C'.

The brief meeting had come to its conclusion and Sally got up from her chair.

"I think enough has been discussed today and I'm sure your anxious to get home to that delicious dinner Indie has cooking. Let me see you out General." Sally said.

Sally led the General by the arm to the patio's sliding glass door. She pulled out a square piece of green marble about two inches in size and half an inch thick attached to a gold chain wrapped around her waist. She pressed a button on it and the glass door disappeared into its recess cut into the wall. Inside the ninety-foot hall, the General looked up into the corner of the castle's family room and saw the crystal, about the size of a baseball, glow red as it received instructions from the control console in Sally's hands.

Crystal was specially crafted using tools invented from thousands of years ago. This was an ancient craft requiring special education. Crystal was cut with the grain, using sound waves to hold it together. This was the most effective way for it to absorb ultra violet rays from the sun and to store and safely release them.

Zen thought the family room was decorative with red and blue tapestry. It featured a Zapatsaur and rider arriving over village'B' just above the domed school and pyramids used for science and education.

The long hallway had a white marble floor just like the family room which continued through the castle's lower level. The hallway was fifteen-feet wide and the ceiling reached up to twenty feet. Crystal lamps mounted on the upper portion of the white marble wall are decoratively fashioned as imitation torch mounts which lean out from the wall by thirty degrees all the way down the hall, on both walls, spaced ten feet apart.

There footsteps echoed down the hall until Sally stopped by the horse shoe shaped entrance to the kitchen.

"I have to check the new calendar. Mitch and Tamara are using this for their mission and some of our trading partners are using this Gregorian calendar you brought us." Sally said.

Zen remembered acquiring this for the family from a trading mission which required military participation heading south past their enemy's island and into pirate dominated waters.

"What's the date today in the outside world." He asked.

"It's February 20, 1688. We're sending copies of the new calendar to our shippers so they won't arrive in the middle of a festival and be unable to unload our goods until its completion. Some of our trading partners are using it now but not all. It's something our shippers will have to keep an eye on." Sally finished.

The General thought about some of the shipping vessels they used to trade produce and crafted goods with their trading partners. Azorka's craftsmen and shipbuilders were expert at duplicating the ships of the seventeenth century. But that's where the similarity ended. Each of these finely crafted ships were equipped with laser cannons and a backup crystal powered motor in the stern of the ship. They were a deadly adversary for pirates to challenge.

"Will the King and Queen be back at the end of the month? The General asked.

"Yes, they had planned to be back by the end of the month. That's what they told me before they left." Sally answered.

The General knew that when they return he would be busy preparing military solutions for the problems they had discovered. Solutions that would counter the new threats that the Empire have devised. Hopefully the Wizard has not advanced their laser technology.

Azorka had a responsibility to keep the Empire from attacking the outside world. Equally challenging would be keeping this technology away from the outside world. If they knew of laser technology and where it was produced, it was feared they would swarm both islands in order to steal it. Azorka was worried about the Empire accidentally giving away the locations of both islands.

Sally left the kitchen and resumed her hold on the General's arm as she led him down the echoing hallway. The ten-foot tall four-foot wide door was beautifully hand carved to suit some of the population that were taller than six-foot. One out of every ten people in Azorka were between seven to ten-feet tall.

Sally moved along the polished marble floor, her white robe flowing over each tile. They reached the door and she pulled out her small marble control console and pressed the button allowing the door to slide into its recess. The wind had picked up and some of the bushes in the front yard were swaying back and forth.

Outside the sun was pouring down on a beautifully landscaped front yard. The Generals Zapatsaur had found a generous snack in Sally's garden. It was a large garden and grown to serve frequently arriving Zapatsaurs for those various officials and diplomats in the community. The General's Zapatsaur was the same size as Sally's Zapatsaur. However, the General's Zapatsaur had emerald green specks of color on all the grey segments of its body and Sally's had red specks of color. Some people thought the Zapatsaur's mouth resembled that of the Komodo Dragon. But unlike the Komodo Dragon, the Zapatsaur has three half-moon shaped solid bone segments which run down its neck, and incredibly alert ears somewhat similar in appearance to those of a wolf. It was rare, but sometimes the Zapatsaur could grow as large as eighteen-feet.

The General's Zapatsaur raised its powerful long neck and turned its head in greeting. It still held a head of lettuce in its three-digit hand and quickly devoured it. A long tail swept some loose rocks out of the way as it prepared for the General to mount. A swift breeze swept some of the General's hair aside on his forehead as he approached, revealing a prominent scar from a battle wound he had received from the Dragon Queen on his last encounter with her. He mounted his Zapatsaur kneeling on its back and grasping the last bony segment on its neck, and looked back at Sally standing on the front porch.

"I'll contact you immediately if there are any more sightings of the Dragon Queen. If not, I'll see you again on the thirtieth with a full report." The General shouted over the wind.

"Thank you, General. I look forward to seeing you again." Sally shouted back over the wind. She turned and entered the castle closing the ten-foot door behind her.

Zen looked up at the enormity of the megalith castle. It rose up one-hundred and fifty-feet and cast a large shadow in the afternoon sun. Made of concrete, marble and wood it was a structural marvel, that could easily accommodate one-hundred guests per social function.

There were fifty rooms each with vaulted ceilings, ten-foot doors and about eight-hundred square feet of living space, lavishly furnished. Downstairs the living room for entertaining guests, which Sally would have walked pass on her way to the kitchen was about seventy-feet in length. Beside this room, across the hall, was a luxuriously furnished dining room where up to fifty guests could be served at its huge oak dinner table. The dining room walls gleamed with the fine polished mahogany selected from the finest forests in the world. Some walls in the castle were covered in marble and others were hung with tapestry which often depicted Azorka's historical events. Overhead but out of sight, the castle's seventy-foot wide roof ran at a forty-five-degree angle and was colored grey. The castles exterior walls were covered in white marble and featured large recessed windows.

The General shook himself free from day dreaming and leaning forward, grasping the bony segment on the Zapatsaurs neck, they rose into the afternoon sky. A strong wind brushed the Generals cap as the Zapatsaur accelerated to a cruising speed of thirty miles per hour. He looked back at the castle. From this height it was the size of his hand. At about four-hundred feet the Zapatsaur levelled off until it was over village'A'. The General wanted to have a quick look at the village to be sure that all appeared normal.

The homes and shops below in the village closest to the castle were domed with an extremely durable and high polished glass which allowed for solar heat and a view free from obstruction for the occupants. Glass was specially treated and submerged in a chemical which would change the glass to a flexible and unbreakable state allowing the builder to form it into a dome.

The hustle and bustle of shoppers moving in and out of irregularly shaped retail and domed produce shops with their Zapatsaurs walking upright with them revealed that all was normal in Village'A'. In another minute he was approaching the border between village'A' and village'B'. The forest was becoming denser, but he could still see the well-guarded secret factories and domed industrial shops hidden there. All was peaceful in village'A'.

The dense old growth forest made it difficult to see but every now and then when the General looked down, he could see a small pyramid or domed building. The Zapatsaur accelerated to fifty miles per hour and was heading to the east coast of village'B' where the General's home was located at the end of the neighborhood closest to the ocean.

Beyond the General's village, a further fifteen miles south, a small grouping of mountains was home to the Zapatsaurs. It was situated like a center piece for Azorka, its many caves serving as homes for the Zapatsaur's. Each home was furnished intelligently for their comfort. But what never ceased to amaze the General was the Zapatsaur's telepathy. The Zapatsaur had always selected its rider as though their mental connection was somehow compatible. The General knew as soon as his Zapatsaur dropped him off it would leave for its home and return the next day when it knew the General needed its help.

The Zapatsaurs were popular throughout Azorka. Including those residents who were not selected by this intelligent animal as riders. A hammock for the Zapatsaur's rest and a garden with food and fresh water was available in every front or backyard on the island. On certain nights, if the hunt went well, then the islands residents would cook up the oversupply of grouse as a special treat for the Zapatsaur. For some unexplained reason the Zapatsaur didn't hunt. However, the Zapatsaur did fish for its dietary requirements. But nothing in the ocean tasted as good as grouse. The Azorkans also treated and mended their injuries in a hospital wing dedicated to them.

The General looked over his shoulder and could see that the storm was approaching. Overhead dark clouds were casting shadows in his neighborhood. He looked down at his home from a height of three-hundred feet as his Zapatsaur began to descend. The homes and buildings in this village sheltered the majority of the island's military.

The General was beginning to relax and looking forward to the company of his wife when at one hundred-feet from his backyard he noticed that something was wrong. On closer examination he saw the Zapatsaur's hammock was sliced in the middle and hanging down in two tattered halves brushing the ground. His garden was trampled. The General got down from his Zapatsaur and walked over to the garden. He looked back over his shoulder and saw his Zapatsaur departing into the cloudy afternoon sky and felt sorry that it couldn't lay in his hammock for a short rest. Suspecting an intruder, the General raced up to his circular domed home and made his way to the front living room window where he was able to see Indie inside. He was relieved that she was safe. He returned to his garden and there he saw the unmistakable foot print of the Dragon Queen, had ruined his crops.

The General took off his hat and wiped sweat from his forehead. He looked up into the cloudy sky at a couple of soldiers, one-hundred-feet above him, arriving home on their Zapatsaurs. He waved up at them and they waved back. He was sure that his home would be the only one affected by what must be a deliberate targeting by the Dragon Queen. An arrogant and daring vandal seeking to aggravate him at his home.

The General made his way up the walk to his home. and opened the front door. All was quiet and when he walked into the hallway, he saw his lovely wife drawing the inside panels. She turned the hand-sized white wheel mounted on the wall of the hallway, drawing the inside panels over the dome above which provided some privacy at night. She turned and smiled as the General walked over and planted a light kiss on her cheek. She looked up at Zen with her large almond shaped brown eyes brushing her raven black hair from her forehead.

"How did your meeting go with the Princess." Indie asked.

Zen had already decided not to mention the damaged hammock and trampled garden.

"It went well Indie. The Princess wants me to keep an eye out for suspected breaches of the Kingdoms security. The usual stuff." Zen replied nonchalantly.

"How did your day go while I was gone." He asked.

"Just a slow day with my usual cleaning chores inside." She said.

Looking in the direction of the kitchen she said,"I made a grouse and vegetable pie and it's about finished cooking now."

Indie walked into the kitchen with Zen following close behind. The kitchen was glowing in the yellow light provided by the amber crystal mounted up high in a corner. Indie opened the oven door and the room filled with a most delicious aroma. Zen's mouth was beginning to water.

"Wow, does that ever smell good." He said.

Indie carried the large pot of grouse pie and set it down at the end of the room on the orange marble kitchen table...Zen walked over and sat down at the table. He reached into the pot with his spoon serving up the delicious dinner as Indie joined him at the table and did the same. A wide smile of accomplishment broke across her face and raising her voice slightly she said,"Perfection." Indie delighted in each delicious mouthful of her successful creation. Her beautiful dark ebony skin glowed brightly in the amber light and she suddenly laughed as she saw Zen spill gravy down the front of his white shirt.

"This is very good. A very tasty dish." the General said as he looked up to see Indie smiling at him.

Indie blushed a little from Zen's compliment.

"Thank you Zen, but it is a modest creation in comparison to what I'm learning to prepare at the school." Indie taught her craft as a seamstress at one of the island's community schools. She also took courses there to learn other skills.

"I'm glad things are going well at the school." the General casually returned.

"I can still teach my course late in the day because there is no need to change the school schedule." Indie said. She watched as Zen shovelled more stew into his mouth.

Indie's ancestors had come from the eastern part of the world and had settled in the northern regions of old Azorka thousands of years ago before the war when there was one great continent that contained the most advanced technologies in the world. With the arrival of people from different cultures all over the world came new ideas and technological advances were rapid. Unfortunately, success encouraged greed and greed fed evil. This developed into the worst possible outcome and that was war.

Azorkan residents in the north wanted to offer the rest of the world, technologies that would prevent suffering from disease as well as other health advances that would promote longer life. They also wanted to offer clean and efficient energy. In stark contrast, the residents in the south of old Azorka wanted to take over the rest of the world, denying health advances so that the worlds population would not become to great. They also wanted to tax crystal powered energy so that they could profit through the use of a clean form of energy.

The result of this conflict was war and it cost both residents in the north and those in the south to lose an equal share of land and advanced technology. The once great continent broke into two islands and the war continues to this day.

Zen finally finished all he could eat and wiping is mouth clean with a napkin, he looked over at Indie. She was deep in thought somehow sensing that her husband needed rest.

"I just realized that we can sleep in tomorrow morning. Now that's a happy reminder and cause for a little celebration." Zen said.

He got up from the table and walked to the other end of the room where the kitchen sink and fridge were. He opened the fridge and grabbed some ale to drink. Looking out the kitchen window at the ocean he noticed that the waves had grown in size with the arrival of the storm.

"I'm looking forward to a little rest. For some reason, I sleep soundly when it's raining. I've had an exhausting day, Indie."

But little did he know how busy tomorrow was going to be.

CHAPTER 2

That early evening the General retired at approximately the same time the King and Queen were making a shocking discovery.

Mitch and Tamara had set sail from the southern tip of Azorka on a secret mission under the cover of darkness the night before. The next day was spent arriving at the northern tip of the Empire's island. The crew included Captain Silverbeard, as he was known to Azorka's trading partners throughout the world, and four crew members who were skilled at sailing this large fishing boat as it was made up to appear. Well-hidden was a laser cannon and the ships backup crystal powered motor concealed in the stern.

Below deck two Zapatsaurs were resting on blankets in the hold, well hidden from sight. They were waiting to carry Mitch and Tamara, at nightfall into the Empire's kingdom. The crew were looking at the shore and surrounding barren looking countryside, from the port side rail. They were anchored five hundred yards from shore. The first mate noticed a few palm trees and other tropical plants on the shoreline that, he thought, just didn't seem to belong there.

Unlike Azorka, which was surrounded by rock and reef sheltering from attack and concealing the Kingdom, the Empire's island was open to invasion. However, there were no buildings crops or any other sign of civilization visible on this seventy-mile long and fifty-mile wide island. No one had thought to profit from an invasion. The islands residents were concealed in caves in the earth. Those underground homes were domed twenty-feet below the surface, still allowing in a small amount of sunlight. They featured a sliding cover which would cover over should they notice uninvited visitors. Some of the residents lived deeper in the earth in a very modern metropolis complete with all of life's necessities, pleasures, and recreation. In 1688, they would be considered an advanced civilization of forty thousand. Like Azorka, their birth rate had been stagnant for centuries. The low birth rate kept pace with the death rate. And forty thousand like-minded residents refused to join the outside world untill it was subdued.

On the top deck of the ship, Mitch and Captain Silverbeard, both dressed in dark clothing, were surveying the Empire's hillside and shore. Beside the Captain, Mitch towered over him by one foot. Mitch was seven-foot-tall and a large athletically built man with short brown hair. He had let his facial hair grow for this mission, looking very much like a pirate with a goatee and mustache. He could be a formidable opponent in combat but was also a kind King for Azorka and his family.

Captain Silverbeard, is a well-respected shipper and sailor for Azorka. His weather beaten face the result of many adventures on the ocean waters. His long grey beard reached down to the first button on his navy-blue shirt and his thick grey hair was covered with a dark cloth hat for this mission. He watched the shoreline in silence while Mitch surveyed the hillside.

Mitch was looking at the Empire's island while the last dim light of a colorful dusk sank into the sea. He was about to lower the telescope when a bright flash from the distant hill caught his attention. He looked through the telescope again and a stream of fire, lit up the hillside. Straining his eyes, he saw a dark silhouette gliding in the evening sky. It was by his estimate, an incredible forty-feet long with a huge wing span propelling it in what looked like a vicious pursuit of its prey. So, Mitch swung the telescope well ahead of the monstrosity in the westerly direction it was traveling. To his surprise and horror, he saw two Zapatsaurs, who shouldn't be there in the first place, were the intended victims. In the next instant the monsters huge reptilian head crept into Mitch's view and the Zapatsaurs were hit by flame shooting out in a deadly stream between the monster's hideously sharp teeth. Both Zapatsaurs were engulfed in the monster's flame and plummeted to the earth below briefly lighting up the darkened landscape like a dying bonfire. Mitch watched the two Zapatsaurs and felt the pain of their agony as they writhed about in torment in their final moments. Finally still, their bodily fluids eventually leaked out into the fire cloaking their carcass leaving two smoking shapes dead in the shallow valley beneath a small hill. Mitch was standing high enough on deck to witness what would haunt him for many years to come. Suddenly, Mitch felt panic, thinking that possibly the two Zapatsaurs in the ships hold had ventured out on their own. He passed the telescope to Captain Silverbeard beside him who had seen the incident, albeit in less detail, and was just standing there in stunned amazement. His eyes were sharp enough that he almost didn't need the telescope.

Mitch ran down the stairs from the Captain's upper command deck to the main deck and called out for Tamara."Tamara, check the Zapatsaurs below." he whispered loudly when he saw her standing close by to the stairs. Tamara raced down the lower deck until she reached the hatchway for the hold. Reaching down and opening one half of the hatchway, she peered inside. A small beam of moonlight poured down through the open hatch and she saw two Zapatsaurs peacefully sleeping on blankets below, unaware of the commotion from above.

Tamara turned to Mitch who had joined her at the hatchway.

"Their sleeping peacefully on our blankets."

Tamara lowered the hatch gently, not wanting to disturb their sleep and walked back over to Mitch who was by the guard rail staring at the Empire's island. She looked up at Mitch and saw that the effects of this shocking experience had put a grim expression on his face.

"What was that sudden explosion of light coming from the island." Tamara asked, expecting bad news.

Mitch looked down at his lovely, mid-aged wife. She was always there for him whether covering his back in a mission or at home as a wife and mother of his children. Her bravery had never faltered when on a mission. Tamara was skilled in combat, her five-foot nine-inch frame a powerhouse when the situation required brute strength.

"I was looking at the island through the telescope and I saw a giant forty-foot flying creature that must have been one of the Wizard's creations. It was chasing a couple of fleeing Zapatsaurs and when it caught up to them it shot a stream of fire from its mouth and covered both Zapatsaurs in flames. They both fell from the sky landing behind a small hill and burnt to death."

Mitch finished his report then he seemed to shake off his state of shock.

"Let's go up top and see what Silverbeard can tell us about this creature. Maybe he'll agree that this creature must have been created by the Wizard, or maybe he's seen a creature like this in another part of the world."

Mitch and Tamara moved swiftly up the stairs to the upper deck where they could already here a conversation in progress. A couple of crew members were discussing what they had seen with Captain Silverbeard.

"Captain" bellowed Dan the first mate, his bald head glowing in the moonlight. "We've seen the most incredible thing with the crew telescope not more than ten minutes ago. There was a flying monster of incredible size breathing out from its mouth a stream of fire." Dan finished, his eyes wide with excitement.

The next crewmate, John, was as wild-eyed with the experience. He was as stout as Dan but had a full head of disheveled red hair.

"I saw the monster and I swear it was large enough to cover the entire lower deck. With lightning speed, it caught up with the Zapatsaurs and killed them." John looked as though he was in shock from the experience.

Captain Silverbeard wanted to avoid panic on his ship and provide his men with some assurance.

looking at both crew

"Now let's not panic. We have the laser cannon available for unwanted monsters." he said members with a stern expression that demanded calm. Then he turned and saw that Mitch and Tamara had arrived and breathed a sigh of relief.

"Mitch and Tamara, you've arrived on time for our discussion. I'm glad to see you."

A relieved look was lighting up his expression, the deep furrows on his forehead disappearing.

Mitch stopped at the entrance to the upper deck, Tamara next to him, and addressed the three men.

"Tamara and I will leave immediately and investigate the incident. It's unusual for two Zapatsaurs to leave Azorka on their own and travel this distance. What would cause them to risk their lives flying above the Empire's island at night."

"We've brought clothing that should convince the Wizard's sentries, should we run in to them, that our unofficial visit is a search for hidden treasure. But it is just as likely that we would not be

approached, thinking it would be better if we left the island thinking it was deserted."

A confident Tamara joined the conversation. She was determined to find out who was responsible for the brutal murder of two Zapatsaurs. She addressed the crew and though she was positive the Wizard was behind this, she kept that thought to herself.

"We'll leave on the backs of our Zapatsaurs flying high above until the cloud cover breaks providing us with more favorable lighting for a stealthy flight. The residents here are light sensitive and unable to look directly at moonlight. Mitch and I will ride beside the beam of moonlight, ten feet above the water to avoid detection."

Captain Silverbeard decided to offer a backup plan for their approval.

"If things don't work out and you find you're on the run from that fire-breathing creature, I could have the laser cannon in place and aiming towards the shoreline. We'd be able to shoot it down fifty yards from the beach if we stay positioned here. However, if we sail a few miles north of our position, away from the island, it may help to hide us from the monster. If it decided to attack the ship the commotion could attract unwanted attention. It would mean you'd have to travel seven minutes longer at one-hundred miles per hour. Of course, as soon as the monster is in our sights we'd shoot it down."

"That's a good idea Captain. Prepare the laser cannon and move the extra distance. Don't worry about killing the creature. It looks to me like it's one of the Wizard's evil abominations." Mitch said.

Mitch and Tamara turned and descended to the lower deck and opened the hatchway to the ship's hold. Mitch moved aside quick enough to avoid being bowled over by his own Zapatsaur racing to get out. Tamara's Zapatsaur was right behind and scrambling up the steps to get out. Both Zapatsaurs moved into flight position on the lower deck, then stood still as statues while waiting for Tamara and Mitch.

They dressed in the dingy light of the ship's hold, where blankets are strewn about the floor and fish nets wreaking of fish from the days catch hung on the planks of the ship's hull. Tamara worked her long dark hair into a pony tail, put on buccaneer boots, and a long black dress with a black cape. Mitch put on a blue undershirt beneath his long dark coat. His sword had a strip of copper worked into the metal designed especially for the Dragon Queen. Tamara had a modest sword strapped around her waist and a small laser derringer, powerful enough to topple a building.

After about five minutes Mitch and Tamara had finally finished dressing. Mitch looked over at Tamara and thought she looked too beautiful to be a Pirate but he wasn't about to tell her that.

"Are you ready for tonight's mission."

"I'm ready to blast some monsters and clobber that Wizard. Let's go do this." she answered.

With that high-spirited affirmation, they climbed the stairs in silence and walked over to their Zapatsaurs waiting on the deck. They were airborne in a couple of minutes rising slowly into a night sky with some clouds occasionally covering the moonlight. Mitch looked down at the ship from one-hundred yards up and saw the crew bustling about. He looked around and ahead into the night watching for any sign of the flying monster. He glanced down at the ship again and saw Captain Silverbeard going into his cabin. Still no sign of the monster. The crew had lowered the sails to catch the remaining wind of the night and were slowly moving in a northerly direction. After a short while Mitch and Tamara were two-hundred yards above the water. Mitch looked down at the ship sailing slowly north, looking no larger than a match box size toy from above. Distance would grant them some invisibility.

Tamara surveyed the land ahead with the telescope, checking for sentries on the beach or countryside. There wasn't any movement or activity and no sign of the flying monster. She looked over at Mitch and pointed down to the water ten-feet left of the trail of light the rising moon had shone towards the Empire's island. Tamara led the way and they both slowly descended until they were in position ten feet above the water. They gradually made their way towards the island at a cautious thirty-miles per hour. The Empire's population had difficulty handling sunlight and moonlight, as they spent so much time underground. Bright light was painful but not lethal. To get around this problem the Wizard had formulated a type of plastic from natural ingredients, that could be used in the production of eye glasses. Tonight's moonlight was just bright enough that an intruder could sneak up to the island by riding just outside of the moonbeam and not be detected. Even the Wizards special eye glasses wouldn't help a sentry detect their movements.

Tamara looked up into the night sky and could see a bank of dark clouds were about to cover the moon. She flew in closer to Mitch and called out over the wind.

"Clouds above are about to cover the moon."

Mitch looked above just in time to see the moon being blocked out by a bank of dark clouds. With the absence of the moonlight, their movement across the water would be more obvious if a sentry was glancing their way from shore. They both came to a stop, hovering above the water. In a couple of minutes, the clouds had passed by the moon and they resumed their slow flight towards shore. The changing rhythm of their Zapatsaurs wings let them know they were close to shore and in the next minute a dark bank loomed up ahead surrounded by a sandy beach which sparkled in the moonlight. They both swooped in quickly landing on the beach. The Zapatsaurs immediately folded their wings to their back and crouched down beneath the bank of land on the beach. Mitch and Tamara did the same. Tamara passed the telescope to Mitch and he looked about confirming that this location was roughly a couple hundred yards away from where the Zapatsaurs remains would be.

"It's two hundred yards to that clearing up ahead and the small hill. There's a shallow valley where the Zapatsaurs remains should be. The four of us will carry on by foot until we're at the crest of the small hill."

The Zapatsaurs led the way. They fell to a crouching position and with great stealth they made their way up a path that divided banks of leafless trees on their right from a field of brown grass on their left. Mitch then Tamara followed behind. Mitch occasionally glanced up at the sky looking for any sign of the fire breathing monster. They kept to the shadows and when they arrived at the crest of the small hill they found cover and Mitch took out the telescope. He gazed down at the small valley below and was startled to find the forty-foot monster, wings folded, and almost walking upright, poking around in the remains of the two fallen Zapatsaurs as though expecting to find something. Mitch was about sixty feet away laying down in the tall grass of the hill and could see the monster's scales were black. Its mouth hung partially open and those deadly needle-sharp teeth caught the moonlight and glistened. The monster looked around as though sensing a presence and its large nostrils issued tendrils of smoke. Mitch turned to Tamara, crouched down beside him.

"Stay down and out of sight. That monster is bellow." he whispered.

Tamara lay flat in the shadows well covered in her black outfit. Both Zapatsaurs were motionless shielded by a tree and tall grass. Mitch could feel the earth shake with every footfall from the monster below. The tree that their Zapatsaurs huddled behind was shaking and small dead branches fell to the ground beside them. Suddenly it abandoned its strange search and took to the sky flying at an incredible speed and clearing another hill above, winging its way in the direction of the Wizard's castle. When all was clear, Mitch and Tamara mounted their Zapatsaurs and flew down a short distance to their fallen friends remains.

Mitch examined the bodies of the murdered Zapatsaurs but couldn't find a logical explanation for the monster's morbid preoccupation with the badly burnt remains. He dug two shallow graves just deep enough to contain their carcasses, giving them a decent burial. After this duty was complete, he looked over to Tamara who was standing close to their Zapatsaurs consoling them by petting their necks. He walked over and with a sympathetic expression he hugged both Zapatsaurs. He looked at Tamara who was brushing away a lone tear and gaining control of her emotions.

"I've been thinking that our simple covert mission of observe and record and return is going to get a whole lot more complicated." He said.

Tamara looked up into his eyes, her emotions under control. She was more determined now to punish the culprits responsible for this tragedy.

"The Wizard is probably behind the creation of the fire-breathing monster and I'll bet the Dragon Queen arranged for the kidnap of a baby Zapatsaur. That would explain why two Zapatsaurs left the island on their own, knowing that their community would only approve a day time mission for rescue. An emotional decision and gamble by two parents not willing to wait for daylight when it could be too late to rescue their baby from the Wizard's experimentation." Tamara finished.

Mitch was nodding his head in agreement.

"We've known for sometime now that the Wizard wants a baby Zapatsaur's brain for his experiments." he reminded Tamara.

"That's right and what a hideous fate that would be for the infant. I don't blame the parents for embarking on such a dangerous rescue mission. Now it's our turn to rescue the baby." She said.

Mitch and Tamara mounted their Zapatsaurs and rose into the blustery night, following the exact path the monstrosity had taken. The moonlight above shone like a spotlight on a clearing up ahead at the top of the larger hill the monster had cleared on its way to the Wizard's castle. Mitch looked behind at Tamara and pointed at the top of the larger hill, where he planned to land. They set down again and Mitch took out his telescope and looked ahead of their position. In the distance the land stretched out towards three enormous cliffs, their rocky faces and natural erosion sheltering a castle below. A stream of water running out from behind the cliff closest to the ocean, was barely visible in the dim light. What caught Mitch's eye was sudden movement on top of the eastern cliff. He zoomed in with his telescope and saw the Wizard all dressed in grey including his strange cone shaped hat. Their arch enemy was standing on top of a boulder raising his four-foot height to an extra foot. Mitch looked over to the rocky cliff face closest to the ocean and was able to make out a familiar flying figure, most likely the Dragon Queen, entering a cave close to the top of the peaks face. He swung the telescope back and caught the Wizard signaling with his wand. His lady servant was close by and holding a large glass beaker, but Mitch couldn't make out what was contained inside.

"Tamara look at this." Mitch whispered then passed her the telescope.

Tamara took the telescope and was just in time to see the Wizard signaling with his wand and the lady servant gliding off the cliff. She hung in midair, suspended over the castle by a flying pack under her clothing, waiting for another signal from the Wizard. The moon light shone down on her yellow dress. and orange cloak. But, what caught Tamara's attention was the sight of the baby Zapatsaur trapped inside the glass beaker.

Tamara passed the telescope back to Mitch. She had an angry expression, and this worried Mitch. In a mission like this it's the cool heads that prevail.

"I thought so. They kidnapped a baby Zapatsaur. The parents were trying to rescue their child, just like we thought earlier." Tamara whispered in an angry tone. "The baby Zapatsaur is probably on its way down to the castle and the Wizard's laboratory."

Mitch looked through the telescope just in time to see the Wizard mount what looked like a green and yellow flying creature the size of a miniature pony but with extremely long legs. There were a couple of ropes attached to the two horns on its head. He watched as the Wizard tugged on the ropes and the creature galloped off the cliff. It was airborne in the sky and descending smoothly towards the castle two-hundred feet below. The lady servant was not descending so smoothly and Mitch watched as she made her descent in short drops, hovering in place for a few seconds then dropping down again. He noticed the wires that connected to the flying pack hidden underneath her clothing, ran out to a control module she held in her right hand. She touched down below before the Wizard and carried the glass beaker inside the castle. The Wizard landed smoothly thanks to the shock absorbing long legs of his creature and entered the castle allowing his creature to fly off into the night. The creature and the Wizard lacked the mental synchronicity of the Zapatsaur and its rider and would be useless together in combat.

Mitch put down the telescope and turned to Tamara.

"Below us, there's a small forest and after that a field of tall grass. We'll fly down to where that forest ends, just a couple hundred yards short of the castle. It'll provide shelter for the Zapatsaurs so they can rest safely while we move on foot into the field and then to the castle."

Tamara nodded her approval then took the telescope and focusing on the field she noticed a shallow three-foot-wide gully ran to the end of the field. It would provide some cover for their approach.

"Mitch, if we follow the gully on the right side of the field it will help conceal our advance."

Mitch took the telescope and looked down at the gully he had somehow missed.

"You're right I missed that. Once we're out of the field, we can make our way using the crags and protruding rock from the bottom of the cliff face as cover. Then the overgrown vegetation and trees in the castle's backyard will help us arrive at the rear walls of the castle." He whispered.

Tamara listened to Mitch as he whispered his plan. The only thing they couldn't be sure about; where the fire-breathing monster was lurking.

"Then will look for a door or window to enter. The difficult part of the rescue is going room to room in order to find the baby Zapatsaur which will probably be chained in the laboratory." Mitch finished.

"I have the derringer to laser off locks and latches, whatever we encounter, so we can select the entrance we want to use." Tamara reminded Mitch.

"If we encounter opposition in the castle the derringer is silent when fired. Who knows what kind of creature the Wizard might have on guard but this will swiftly and silently destroy it. The only uncontrollable variable is the fire-breathing creature. I almost think my derringer would not be powerful enough to bring it down but I know a laser cannon would." Tamara advised.

Mitch was relieved Tamara was under control and thinking through everything. Not more than fifteen minutes ago she was angry enough to abandon caution and let her emotions take over. A fatal mistake on a mission as dangerous as this had become. He always appreciated Tamara's stability and cool head in difficult situations.

He looked down and smiling said,"It appears that our smallest weapon in the hands of our Queen is the most powerful on this mission."

"I know I don't have to remind you that even the best laid plans are not always fully executed in the operation because of unforeseen circumstances. A good example of that would be the flying monster dive bombing on us while we're in the gully." Tamara whispered over the wind.

"You don't have to remind me. We've been on enough missions together to know that's true."

With that said they both mounted their Zapatsaurs and were flying through the windy night on their way to the edge of the forest where they could hide their Zapatsaurs. Mitch couldn't be sure if deadlier creatures roamed the island at night. He didn't want to risk exposing their Zapatsaurs to danger and they did need to rest.

While in flight Tamara was watching for the flying monster and noticing the rocky and dense vegetation of the Empire's island and thought it would be challenging for even the best hiker. She watched as Mitch looked around from east to west for any sign of the monster. Then Tamara looked down and saw that the forest's tree tops appeared closer. She watched Mitch's Zapatsaur as it brushed some tree tops fifty-feet away from landing in a clearing near the forest's edge. The Zapatsaurs landed and they hopped off. Their Zapatsaurs left them, walking a short distance to a copse of trees to hide under and rest.

Mitch and Tamara set out on foot down the fields gully as planned. A strong wind blew and the sound of the wind rushing through the tall grass of the field helped to cover any noise they might make such as the snapping of a dead branch.

Overhead the moon fought back against an arriving bank of clouds but lost and the field was pitched into darkness giving Tamara and Mitch the advantage of greater invisibility. They got through the field without incident then moved swiftly towards the rocky face of the eastern cliff under the overhanging rock where they could survey the castle and its backyard.

Mitch took out his telescope and pointed it at the castle. He saw that there was a light on in a room that was close to the courtyard. Perhaps, he thought, this was the laboratory where the Wizard was working. There was no movement on the upper walkway for the courtyard and both turrets at the front of the castle were dark. The taller and larger circular tower in the backyard, that was separated from the castle by thirty yards, was dark as well. Mitch put down the telescope and turned to Tamara speaking in a whisper and pointing at the castle's room.

"One light on in the far wing over there. Must be the laboratory"

"Let me see." Tamara whispered back.

She took the telescope, scanning the castle and the approach they must take to get to this room. She whispered her plan to Mitch. They would proceed ahead using the trees and overgrown vegetation as cover. There was a large patch of overgrown vegetation at the corner of the castle's back wall that would conceal them. At this point they would be west of the large tower, it's lights still out and darkened windows capturing a reflection of the moon. Tamara and Mitch would slide along the castle's wall until they found a door or window to laser open.

"Sounds like a good plan to me." Mitch whispered back.

He took the telescope, folded it smaller and attached it to his belt. Mitch was ready for action and focused for stealth. They both moved forward quietly from tree to tree until they reached the castle's rear corner and overgrown vegetation which they could hide in until they were ready to move again.

While Tamara and Mitch had been advancing on the Wizard's castle, Captain Silverbeard and the crew had sailed the necessary distance of a few miles, out of the flying monster's eye shot, and dropped anchor for the night. They were sitting down on the upper deck's starboard side benches and engaged in conversation about recent events. Dan was slouched in the corner, his stout shape and the evening shadows helping to give him the appearance of a parked barrel. He was listening attentively to Captain Silverbeard and his crew mate John discussing some of Azorka's new challenges in their fight against the Empire. The other two crew members were on watch. Jack was at the bow of the ship with the crew's telescope looking for signs of the flying monster. Chuck was on the main deck, using Captain Silverbeard's telescope, covering east and west.

John brushed back a handful of his red hair and said,"So the Empire's crystal technology is so crude we don't have to worry about the flying pack?"

"That's right." Captain Silverbeard returned."The trick with crystal technology is how the crystal is cut. It has to be cut with the grain in order to get the best results. This is accomplished by lowering a clear dome, designed with specially calibrated low-level sound waves, over the crystal. The sound waves hold the crystal together, preventing it from splitting, while the trained artisan cuts the crystal with a laser attached inside the dome. Azorka moved its highly advanced technology underground in village'A' for security reasons after the war. The Empire had the same technology before the war but all of that sank to the bottom of the ocean. Their crystal technology is crude, poorly produced without these special tools. A good example of this inferior technology would be the intel report on their new flying pack. It does not descend or ascend smoothly."

Dan in the corner came to life and said,"But now we have to contend with the Wizard's creature's and they fly fast!"

Captain Silverbeard looked over and smiled reassuringly.

"We have the laser cannon prepared and I'm hoping we get a shot just to see how tough these creatures are."

John piped up and said,"I don't think I care to challenge one until I know for sure what were up against."

"Well that will be up to Mitch and Tamara to learn." Captain Silverbeard replied."Their mission is to collect as much information as possible about the Empire's experiments and advancements."

"Mitch and Tamara are front line monarchs leading the charge in almost every mission. They have confidence in our military and the bravery to succeed in combat. I know Azorka is in good hands. Mitch's seven-foot stature serves him well and I know he's one of the strongest men in our Kingdom, but I don't think he could out wrestle a forty-foot flying fire-breathing reptile." Dan finished.

Captain Silverbeard thought a while then said,"Both Mitch and Tamara are well trained top of their class fighting machines and weapons experts. Let me explain."

Captain Silverbeard told John and Dan that knowledge of the Wizard's creation of hybrid flying creatures and other dangerous life forms prompted greater military solutions. The laser gun was made more powerful and more portable like the derringer Tamara took on this mission. Training had produced aerial acrobatics thanks mostly to the capabilities of the Zapatsaur. Tamara had rehearsed the maneuver several times. This was an offensive military tactic. The Zapatsaur holds the rider in its hands, arms outstretched, moving the rider quickly within one-hundred and eighty degrees of mid-air turning, while the rider fires our most powerful laser gun at the enemy's creature.

The Captain continued to explain that in order to get into position for this maneuver, while in flight, the Zapatsaur would suddenly fold its wings and at this precise moment the rider would jump up in the open air. The Zapatsaur arranged its body vertically as it began to drop then worked its wings again and at the same time caught the rider who was also falling, in its outstretched hands. This aerial acrobatic maneuver is accomplished in less than thirty seconds.

Dan whistled his approval and said,"That does sound slick!

John joined in and said,"That is an extremely complex method of combating flying monsters but I bet it is effective. The rider has an unobstructed view and doesn't have to worry about firing his laser gun around the wings and head of his Zapatsaur. But what about the Wizard's force field that he produced for the Dragon Queen? Could the flying creatures be smart enough to use it?

Captain Silverbeard thought a moment then spoke up.

"I would say the creatures lack the intelligence right now. It has always been our military's concern that the Wizard could change that. Before the war, the Wizard, who we believe is somehow immortal, was the top in his field. He was producing combat monsters up to the very end, just before the firestone sent their Kingdom and ours, to the ocean floor, all two-hundred miles of it. Fortunately, the monster foot soldiers he had produced to fight against us were caught up in the calamity and drowned. At last the world was just a little safer now from the remaining enemy because they were cut off from their most advanced technology. But don't under estimate the Wizard." The Captain finished.

Captain Silverbeard got up from the bench and stretched.

"I'm going to get a little shut eye and I suggest you two do the same before its your turn for watch." Captain Silverbeard walked to his cabin and shut the door.

Back on the Empire's island, Mitch and Tamara had worked out their approach to a rear door just visible past the courtyard back wall. Tamara went first hugging the back wall and moving silently. When she had reached a half-way point along the wall, Mitch followed her footsteps until he caught up to her waiting by the door.

"Are you ready?" Tamara whispered. Mitch gave a nod of this head.

Tamara pulled out the derringer from a pocket in her dress and putting it on a lower setting she aimed it into the doors lock. The door gently swung inwards and Mitch entered first with his sabre drawn as a precaution.

There was no sign of life in the dingy torch lit hall. Tamara, walking behind Mitch, looked at the brick walls covered in a wet slime, most likely caused from the moisture of the ocean. The floors were covered in a dark marble and they were both thankful for the absence of creaking wood boards. The wooden ceiling was vaulted and twenty feet high. It had collected a small amount of soot from each torch in its wall bracket. Mitch and Tamara walked down the twenty-feet of hallway until it opened out into a circular shaped reception area. Here the ceiling rose to thirty-feet and the walls were covered in red and gold tapestry. A few small items of furniture were tucked in various locations around the room and Mitch thought this could be a meeting place or planning room for the Empire's strategic plans concerning world domination. Orange marble floor continued from the hall into this large circular room that probably contained a thousand feet of living space. Beautiful European style area rugs, of the most remarkable quality covered half the marble flooring. Furniture fit for royalty could be seen against the walls and grouped together with exquisitely finished wood tables and needlepoint chairs. At the far end of the room was another corridor that led in the direction of the room with the light on; maybe the laboratory.

Mitch and Tamara crossed the forty-foot long room and made their way down another hallway similar to the first hallway except this one contained a guard. The guard had his back to them. Tamara and Mitch froze on the spot. Mitch noticed a small table behind him and he pulled Tamara back and behind it for cover. Tamara pulled out the derringer and set it on maximum. The plan with this shot was to completely vaporize the guard so that he wouldn't make any noise when taken out. He was guilty by association and involved in the kidnapping, so the taking of his life was permitted. The guard stood silently outside the entrance to a room and as far as Tamara could see he wasn't armed. He was about six-feet tall, had pale skin, and was clothed in the Empire's common textiles, with an animal fur vest and leather boots.

Tamara pulled the trigger and in the next three seconds the guard was covered in a circle of red color before disappearing soundlessly. Both Mitch and Tamara moved swiftly down the hall arriving at the door. It wasn't locked and it was the room with the light on they saw from outside. They entered silently and took up a position behind a small grouping of filing cabinets. They looked around and Mitch spotted a cage in the center of the room with the baby Zapatsaur trapped inside.

Mitch nudged Tamara and she gave a thumb up to let him know that she saw their target for rescue. She noticed a single bead of sweat run down from Mitch's dark brown hair into his mustache and then his goatee. At the far end of the room where a crystal powered set of lights lit up a corner ten-feet by fifteen-feet was a glass enclosure. Inside the Wizard was looking through an old Kingdom microscope that was probably salvaged after the war. His grey cone hat was off and he was oblivious to Mitch and Tamara's presence. Tamara caught something standing upright at the corner of the room about ten-feet away from the Wizard. It was completely motionless, about eight-feet tall and produced a shadow. Tamara figured it was either a statue or decorative pillar and ignored it.

Tamara tapped Mitch on the arm and whispered in his ear.

"I'm going to grab the cage and bring it back here. I'll laser it open and then we can leave without being noticed."

This time it was Mitch's turn for a thumb up.

Tamara moved out into the center of the room and stopped in front of the cage. Her foot falls were silent on the marble floor. Tamara knew, from everything that was known about Zapatsaur development, that the baby Zapatsaur would remain silent and assist the rescue anyway necessary. The Zapatsaurs telepathy was well developed at an early age and it realized that silence would be necessary for a successful escape. Tamara reached out with both arms and slowly and silently she took hold of the cage. She looked in on the infant and could almost swear that it was smiling at her. Tamara moved back swiftly with her fifty-pound prize and placed it down beside Mitch. She took out her laser derringer, changed the setting to 'low' and lasered off the lock. The baby Zapatsaur jumped up into Tamara's arms and Mitch led the way back to the door with Tamara and the infant in her arms following. After closing the door silently, Mitch and Tamara made their way back down the hallway. They arrived at the reception room with its finely crafted wood ceiling and furniture. That's when they heard a bone chilling growl echoing through the hall they had just left, possibly coming from the laboratory. And then they heard the sound of a door crashing open echoing down the hall and into the reception room. They were too far from the first hallway entrance they had used to get inside the castle and wouldn't make it over there on time before being seen. They decided on selecting one of three doors on their right.

Tamara looked at Mitch with a shrug, holding the baby close to her, suggesting he should decide on which door they would try.

"You decide which one." She whispered loudly.

So, Mitch chose the door in the middle and when they closed the door behind them they were standing at the bottom of a circular staircase instead of an exit out into the night like they had hoped. Too late to change their minds and try another door. They climbed upwards by the light of small torches in ornate holders attached to the wall of what was obviously one of the castles turrets. At the top of the stairs a crude but sturdy wooden door led into the turrets only room. A large window allowed a stream of moonlight into the room and as they closed and locked the door behind them they saw that they were facing the front of the castle. The room was circular and had no furnishings. Tamara was looking around the room hoping to find a rope long enough to rappel down the fifty-feet to the bottom sidewalk and escape into the night. No such luck this time.

"Hey Tamara, Mitch called.

He was standing over a couple of flying packs with straps attached to them and a wire and console plugged into the side of each pack.

"I think I've found the Wizard's flying packs."

Tamara with the baby Zapatsaur clinging to her, walked over to see this discovery. But downstairs a commotion was building. Doors were being slammed and voices could be heard shouting orders. The most unearthly sound was the growl coming from one of the Wizard's creature's that must have been on guard duty. When that growl sounded again it was accompanied with a slamming door and Mitch feared the beast had stumbled through the downstairs door. Those fears were realized when Mitch could hear the creature's heavy footfalls on the staircase below.

"Tamara there's no time left. Put on the pack and hold this console for the controls. We've known about these packs for some time and believe that the four buttons on the console are for your direction, north, south, east, west. The center button is up and directly underneath that button is the button for down. Intelligence is not sure if the Wizard has made improvements to the pack, so from what I've seen it could be a rough descent. Wait for me by the Zapatsaurs. I'll be right behind you." Mitch finished.

It was a rushed orientation, but right now the best option for escape. Mitch helped Tamara into the flying pack.

"Before you leap out of the window, I want you to press the up button lightly to confirm it works." Mitch said.

Tamara did that and rose three feet off the floor. She pressed the button below and dropped down gently to the floor. She gave a thumb up and moved towards the window with the baby Zapatsaur clinging to her neck and shoulder. Tamara stepped up to the sill pushing aside a half-opened shutter on the window and looked back at Mitch.

"Here we go."

Tamara smiled back at Mitch and with that she pushed the north and up button at the same time. To her relief the pack responded smoothly and she was disappearing into the darkness, heading in the direction of the resting Zapatsaurs with the rescued baby in her arms.

Mitch knew he had to haul on his flying pack before the creature reached the door. The creature was likely powerful enough to break down the door and if that happened he had to move fast. He could hear the growling and felt the monster's heavy footfalls shaking the room. It was getting closer. The creature must weigh a ton to be causing a vibration on stone steps and he wondered how large this monster was.

Downstairs the Wizard had left his laboratory after reviving his creature and ordering it to pursue and destroy the invaders. The Wizard was furious about the rescue of the baby Zapatsaur. He had been able to advance his experiments progress by extracting a small amount of blood from the baby and now when he had a good idea of how to move forward the specimen was gone. He had raised his head from the microscope in order to stretch and turned around to see the baby Zapatsaurs cage empty on the floor. Some satisfaction lay in the thought of what his creature would do to the invaders.

The large shadow that Tamara had seen in the room was the creature that the Wizard revived from its rest. The Wizard had created a creature that was part wolf and part lizard. He had refrained from giving the creature wings but instead gave it fins on its calves and forearms thinking he could adapt it into an intelligent amphibian someday. So, the Wizard had put this creation to sleep in his laboratory.

The Wizard was in the reception area now and barking out orders to the night time sentries on duty in the castle. They were already running around looking for any sign of the intruders.

"Larry! Check the backyard. The intruders might be in the backyard huddled behind a bush!" He shouted.

"Hodgi! Check the turret opposite to the one my creatures in!"

Upstairs the creature had reached the door to the room and had stopped outside. Mitch was just pulling tight the last strap for the flying pack when there was a loud crash from the creature hitting the wood door that reverberated inside the circular stone room. He looked over at the locked door at the exact instant the creature decided to charge into it from the other side. It buckled, almost warping in its frame, but it held. Mitch decided to pull out his musket pistol. He had seen a square peep window at eye level on the inside of the door that he hadn't noticed before. His curiosity was overwhelming and he decided to give in to it. Mitch walked over to the sliding peep window and opened it peering out into the dimly lit hallway. Mitch should have been paralyzed with fear. Instead he was fascinated by what he saw. A creature that was part wolf and part reptile. It was a foot taller than Mitch and had a long mouth full of razor-sharp teeth. The monster was green in color and had extremely powerful arms and legs with fins attached to them, suggesting that it might be amphibious.

Mitch could see that the barrel of his musket pistol would fit through the peep window, and he was ready to leap into flight. Why not try a quick shot to see if his copper ammunition can stop the monster. He fired and the outside hall filled with smoke and the sound of the gun firing echoed all the way down to the bottom of the stairs.

The Wizard suddenly aware of the gun fire called out to his sentries. He pointed at a couple of leather clad huntsmen.

"You two! The middle door over there! Get up those stairs and find out what's going on! He yelled, his eyes wide with anger.

They both ran to the door, swords drawn.

Mitch should have jumped up onto the window ledge and left but again his curiosity got the better of him. He looked through the peep window to see if the copper shot had been effective. Much to his disappointment the monster was still standing, with a chunk of flesh missing from the left side of its neck. Blood from the wound dripped onto the stone floor staining it a peculiar green color. Mitch concluded that the copper ammunition had no effect on this creature. On the other side of the door the creature ran at the door, throwing all its weight at the door which finally gave in flying open and crashing against the inside wall where Mitch had been a moment earlier. Mitch jumped up onto the window ledge and leaping out into the night, was airborne leaving the monster growling in the window behind him. Mitch took in a breath of fresh air and exhaled some of his anxiety. He was flying fifty feet off the ground and not having any trouble with the flying pack. Maybe the servant girl just needed more practice. But then it was possible that the Wizard may have perfected his flying pack and these were the latest models. Mitch was determined to get these packs back to Azorka's research department.

But for now, Mitch wanted to get back to Tamara and the Zapatsaurs. They would be anxiously waiting for his arrival and concerned about the Wizard mobilizing more of his creatures to chase them. Especially the fire-breathing monster they feared the most.

Mitch was enjoying his ride, actually impressed with the flying pack and its precise response. However, when he came within fifty-yards of the rendezvous point he thought he saw movement about one-hundred yards away in the forest. He landed smoothly in front of Tamara.

"I'm glad to see you. I heard what sounded like your musket going off and then a horrible crash." She said, relieved that Mitch had survived the ordeal.

"I just got away on time. Let's just get out of here and back to the ship. Leave your flying pack on. I want to get this back to our research department for General Zen to look at." He said.

Tamara and Mitch mounted their Zapatsaurs, but before they made their escape Mitch had an idea. He was suspicious of the movement he thought he detected in the forest.

"Pass me the derringer. I think I should ride rear guard while you fly on ahead to the ship." He said. Tamara passed him the laser derringer then rose into the sky and departed with the baby Zapatsaur in her arms. Mitch was about to join her when he heard a rustling of bushes then the pounding of the earth as a huge creature charged towards him. Mitch and his Zapatsaur departed quickly rising into the sky. He looked back and to his astonishment he was being chased by a flying creature that had a striking resemblance to the creature he left behind in the castle.

Mitch's first priority was to protect his Zapatsaur from what might be a fire-breathing creature. The telepathic communication kicked in between Zapatsaur and rider. The Zapatsaur and rider decided on an evasive maneuver by spiraling upwards at a seventy-degree angle and in the opposite direction to that taken by Tamara. The creature tried to follow but lost significant speed in doing so. It lacked the speed and strength necessary to catch up with the Zapatsaur. Mitch's Zapatsaur reached the apex of its climb and at that precise moment Mitch jumped up into the air with his arms spread wide and the Zapatsaur positioned itself in a ninety-degree angle just below him, its wings folded up and beginning to drop. Mitch fell close enough for his Zapatsaur to catch him by the waist with its enormous hands. The Zapatsaur unfolded its wings and both Mitch and his Zapatsaur were ready for battle, now hovering in mid-air. The creature approached them, its needle-sharp teeth visible in the moonlight and rushed at them with both its scaly arms outstretched for the kill. Mitch had selected maximum force on the laser derringer, and opened fire on the monster. The creature was briefly outlined in a red hue then was so completely vaporized that there wouldn't even be dust left behind to testify to its destruction.

Mitch waited, hovering in mid-air for a further five minutes to see if the Wizard would release more creatures. His Zapatsaur rotated in all directions while Mitch used his telescope, prepared for another challenge.

Tamara had arrived on the ship with the baby Zapatsaur around the same time Mitch was completing his survey for more challengers. Tamara called up to Captain Silverbeard and let him know that Mitch had the laser derringer and would arrive shortly. Both the baby Zapatsaur and Tamara's Zapatsaur went into the hold of the ship where they could feed and rest. As Tamara walked up the stairway to the upper deck she heard the excited voices of the crew.

"Captain Silverbeard did you see that." Chuck shouted out, dancing happily from side to side. His thin and lanky body leaned forward and his full head of blonde hair fell into his eyes as he addressed the Captain. The Captain had been surveying the island with his telescope and had witnessed the same bright red flash that Chuck had seen and he knew that Mitch would be returning to the ship shortly. Both Chuck and the Captain knew that Mitch had vaporized a monster and it was a very satisfying feeling.

"Yes, I did, Chuck and if you ask me that was a laser derringer destroying its target. Tamara said she gave the derringer to Mitch." Captain Silverbeard replied with a smile creasing his weather beaten face.

"I'm glad that Mitch asked for my derringer before I left that hideous island." Tamara called out to Chuck and Captain Silverbeard.

Captain Silverbeard and Chuck watched Tamara climb the final step up onto the upper deck.

"Mitch thought it would be best if he took on the creatures that the Wizard might send after us. He was even prepared to face the fire-breathing monster. This was assurance that the baby and I would escape pursuit and the location of our ship would remain secret." Tamara said.

She leaned against the ship's railing and looked in the direction that Mitch would be returning from. Chuck and Captain Silverbeard looked in the same direction and saw the first dim light of dawn starting to rise from the ocean.

"Mitch will probably leave shortly now that the sun is rising. The Wizard's creatures are sensitive to the sun and unless they're wearing the Wizards glasses, I doubt that they'll leave their pens. When Mitch gets back it should be safe to rest a couple of hours before we set sail for Azorka." Tamara said.

A couple minutes after that they heard Jack, the other crew member working on the main deck, calling up to them.

"Mitch is on his way back. He's a couple hundred yards away." Jack shouted. A happy expression washed over his wrinkled face. He held the ships telescope in his right hand.

The Dragon Queen had also watched Mitch leaving the island. She was on her way to the Wizard's castle, before the sunrise, and had stopped long enough to witness the destruction of the Wizard's creature. Never had she seen such a demonstration of laser power, at least not since the war. The Empire had lost all that technology as it sank to the sea during the final days of the war. The finely crafted, rust resistant, laser tool and specially calibrated sound wave inserts, were waiting to be recovered at the bottom of the ocean.

A special future project waiting to be launched by the Wizard would recover the lost technology. An intelligent amphibious creature, capable of withstanding ocean pressures at great depths, would return the lost technology.

Now the Dragon Queen was anxiously seeking assurance that the force field pack she wore would protect her from such a devasting blow. She felt the pack attached to her white belt. So far it has been working well, she thought.

Today she would return the special metal net to the Wizard for safe keeping. It was extremely strong and she had wrapped it around her waist. Both the Wizard and the Dragon Queen had under estimated the size of the firestone and had she gained entry to the bank, she wouldn't have been able to carry it back to the Empire's island.

"The creature was completely vaporized, obliterated! It looked motionless in the air when it was hit by the laser, and enclosed by a red mist, then in the next second it disappeared from sight!" The Dragon Queen shouted at the Wizard as she paced nervously back and forth in front of him in the castle's reception room.

Her wings and two extra arms were folded neatly behind her back but her green forehead perspired copiously. Even her large reptilian feet left perspiration marks on the marble tiles.

The Wizard sat on his favorite needle-point chair and listened to the Dragon Queen with an expression of concern, for her benefit. He had known her since she was a young child named Maria. She had always been fearless even before the lab experiment which she had agreed to. He knew that practically no power in the Universe could cause his force field to fail except copper. For some reason the force field was useless against a projectile made of copper.

"I understand your need for assurance. The force field is the best protection I can give you presently. Even the superior laser technology you witnessed, would not be able to penetrate this shield. However, copper can penetrate the force field. Now you know that a copper tipped arrow is not going to be lethal. Believe me Maria I'm doing everything I can to work on this problem we have with copper." The Wizard said with confidence hoping to calm down the Dragon Queen.

The Dragon Queen stopped pacing and stood in front of the Wizard. She was amazed at how calm and confident he was after seeing the damage from the chaos the intruders created by rescuing the baby Zapatsaur. The castle's front turret had a ruined door, shattered to pieces by the creature. This abominable creation had a serious intelligence deficit and leapt out the turret's window landing on its head and now it lay in a heap below. It was obvious how badly the Wizard required the Zapatsaur genetics as it might provide a short cut to a problem he had been trying to solve for years now.

The Wizard looked into the Dragon Queen's fiery eyes. The pupils were beginning to change and they looked more elongated. He made a mental note to watch this new development although it had taken ten-thousand years to become noticeable. He looked deep into her eyes, suggesting that her irrational outburst was a paranoid reaction, an unnecessary consideration, and that she was safe. The Dragon Queen was starting to feel better. She could hear the howl of a creature caught outside under the stinging rays of the sun. It would fly swiftly to a nearby cave for relief from the sun and rest from its nightly patrol.

The Dragon Queen was upset that the specimen had been rescued. She wondered if the Wizard would feel better howling about his loss. She knew it wasn't a good idea to bottle up your frustrations. Planning an attack against Azorka might relieve some of that agony. It would be a wise consideration. The sharp and shrewd intelligence the Wizard had known the Dragon Queen possessed gave her an idea that there was an easier way to accomplish their objectives.

The Dragon Queen, suddenly energized by her plan drew closer to her four-foot accomplice. He was to relaxed sitting there on his luxuriously sphalend and crafted European chair. His short legs dangled above a crimson colored hand-woven carpet. But that calm composure changed as he heard the Dragon Queen's plan. A wicked smile broke out and his dark, navy blue eyes seemed to light up with joy.

CHAPTER 3

Mitch's arrival was a welcome sight for all. Mitch and Tamara had rescued the baby Zapatsaur and had recovered two of the Wizard's flying packs for Azorka's research department. They knew what kind of creature's the Wizard was creating and that he had plans to create an amphibious creature. They decided to abandon the rest of the mission. The invasion had been discovered, the infant rescued, so the Wizard would be on high alert.

Mitch and Tamara had decided to retire with the Zapatsaurs where the darkness of the ship's hold would shield them from the daylight sun. They didn't bother to change out of their seventeenth century clothing, styled and produced in the outside world. Mitch rested his head against a stack of coiled rope and looked over at Tamara who had found comfort on a blanket.

"We have to get back and plan a major assault on the Wizard and his castle. It would be nice to put his laboratory out of business. He's dangerously close to being a threat to both Azorka and the world. If the Wizard was able to extract enough biological information and blood from the Zapatsaur then he could be that much closer to creating a smart creature." Mitch whispered, not wanting to disturb the sleeping Zapatsaurs.

"I agree with that. Things on the Empire's island have spun out of control. Probably won't be long before a ship from the outside world sails by at night and spots one of these fire-breathing creatures lighting up the landscape." She whispered with a quick smile briefly hiding her exhwsted expression.

"I can hardly wait to tell Sally and Heather about their father stealing the show and lasering the Wizard's creature. You did great with my derringer." Tamara whispered.

Mitch watched her eyes fluttering as she struggled to stay awake.

"It has remarkable power for such a small laser weapon. The men and women in military research are doing incredible work with our crystal technology. We are getting closer to the sophisticated craftsmanship which produced the Firestone thousands of years ago." Mitch said as he looked over and saw that Tamara was still awake and listening.

Mitch carried on with the conversation.

"We have to stop the Wizard from producing any more of those monsters. If we're not careful we could find ourselves overwhelmed with his creations. He'd use Azorka as his first test. If he could defeat us, the rest of the world would be a snap. When he defeats the world's armies with those monsters, the Empire will be able to control the entire planet."

Mitch looked over at Tamara who was now sound asleep. In another five minutes so was Mitch.

The Dragon Queen left the Wizard who was shouting out orders to his staff to clean up after the invaders. She was furious after all the trouble she went through in order to kidnap a baby Zapatsaur. Even that had been a partial failure with the Zapatsaur parents in hot pursuit. All she could think of was being gored by those hideous three-digit feet. Like her own, with three-inch sharp claws and the same size as her own but with at least three times the weight behind each thrust. And they were angry, in hot pursuit at one-hundred miles per hour across the water. The Dragon Queen could barely stay ahead of them while the baby Zapatsaur struggled against her grip. Fortunately, the Wizard had rescued the mission by dispatching his largest and most vicious creature, this one capable of projecting a stream of fire from its mouth. When she looked back those two Zapatsaurs were engulfed in flames and falling to the ground below.

After discussing the mission with the Wizard, she was finally back in her cave in the uppermost peak that looked down from a distance on the Wizard's castle. She found her dark glasses. They were hanging by a strap on the roughhewn rock wall inside her cave. Beside the glasses hung the specially crafted laser gun that she had used on the door to Azorka's bank. She looked down at the comfort of her twelve-foot softly padded couch and knew that she would appreciate the rest when the newly hatched plan was complete. This, she thought, should shake up those arrogant Azorkans. She put on the special glasses that would protect her eyes, giving her the freedom to travel in the daylight. No more complicated than a couple of oval dark lens fit into a thin metal frame that hung over her eyes and secured by a strap that wrapped around her head. Now, she thought to herself, I look more like a large insect than a reptilian-human hybrid. She walked back out to the entrance to her lair, looking out on a bright and sunny day through the protection of her dark glasses. Without further hesitation she launched into the morning sky and in another minute, she reached a speed of one-hundred miles per hour which would have her touching down in Azorka two hours from now.

While Mitch and Tamara slept, Azorka was waking up to a rich blue sky filled with sunshine. The General Zen was up early, well before Indie and had cleaned up the evidence of that unwelcome visit from the Dragon Queen. The torn hammock was replaced with a slightly different color. It only took another fifteen minutes to clean up the garden. Indie would never know their most feared enemy could be so close and he would arrange for more neighborhood security with copper arrows to repel any further visits. After these duties had been completed and after the General sent out special orders for more sentries to guard his neighborhood of mostly military families, he mounted his Zapatsaur, which had arrived just five minutes ago. The General flew south to the mountains that were home to the Zapatsaur population.

Back at the castle, Sally and Heather were in the kitchen having breakfast.

"We're going to have an excellent crop of blueberries this year." Heather said. She shovelled an over generous spoonful of blueberries into her mouth. The blueberries had been drenched in a bowlful of maple syrup. Heather's beautiful hazel eyes closed in a brief moment of breakfast joy as her taste buds reacted to the delicious morning breakfast treat.

"What about the broccoli this year. Sally enquired. This was Sally's favorite vegetable and she remembered how good last year's crop was.

"There is no reason to think it wouldn't be as successful as last year except it is warmer this year than last year. We can change the harvest date without affecting the quality." Heather finished. She brushed back her dark brown hair over her shoulder. Sally laughed as another lock of Heather's hair fell into her blueberry bowl. Heather picked it out of her bowl, dripping with maple syrup and brushed it away with a brief expression of frustration.

"You know what's going on tonight, Heather." Sally asked.

Heather looked up from her bowl and suddenly her eyes lit up.

"That's the barbeque tonight in village 'B', I almost forgot. All our friends from school will be there." She happily answered.

While Mitch and Tamara slept, Azorka was waking up to a rich blue sky filled with sunshine. The General Zen was up early, well before Indie and had cleaned up the evidence of that unwelcome visit from the Dragon Queen. The torn hammock was replaced with a slightly different color. It only took another fifteen minutes to clean up the garden. Indie would never know their most feared enemy could be so close and he would arrange for more neighborhood security with copper arrows to repel any further visits. After these duties had been completed and after the General sent out special orders for more sentries to guard his neighborhood of mostly military families, he mounted his Zapatsaur, which had arrived just five minutes ago. The General flew south to the mountains that were home to the Zapatsaur population.

Back at the castle, Sally and Heather were in the kitchen having breakfast.

"We're going to have an excellent crop of blueberries this year." Heather said. She shovelled an over generous spoonful of blueberries into her mouth. The blueberries had been drenched in a bowlful of maple syrup. Heather's beautiful hazel eyes closed in a brief moment of breakfast joy as her taste buds reacted to the delicious morning breakfast treat.

"What about the broccoli this year. Sally enquired. This was Sally's favorite vegetable and she remembered how good last year's crop was.

"There is no reason to think it wouldn't be as successful as last year except it is warmer this year than last year. We can change the harvest date without affecting the quality." Heather finished. She brushed back her dark brown hair over her shoulder. Sally laughed as another lock of Heather's hair fell into her blueberry bowl. Heather picked it out of her bowl, dripping with maple syrup and brushed it away with a brief expression of frustration.

"You know what's going on tonight, Heather." Sally asked.

Heather looked up from her bowl and suddenly her eyes lit up.

"That's the barbeque tonight in village'B', I almost forgot. All our friends from school will be there." She happily answered.

Sally looked up from her light breakfast of toast and smiled, thinking of the fun they would have.

"There will be the games just like last year. That includes the racket games with the feathered ball each team sends over the net back and forth. You remember last year how your team won the second racket game that's played with the light ball on the concrete court. The music is also a treat. We have so many talented musicians here in Azorka."

Heather was thinking back to last year's village barbeque.

"That was a blast of fun. You reminded me of how excited we all were after winning the second game. The barbeque itself was really fantastic with all those different varieties of meat from the outside world." Heather's mouth was beginning to water.

"So, there you go. We've got something fun to do tonight." Sally said.

Heather's expression was radiant but then it suddenly took on a quizzical look.

"I wonder what young people around the outside world will be doing tonight."

Sally was two year's older than Heather with shoulder length light brown hair. But despite slight physical differences, like Sally being half an inch taller, family resemblance was unmistakable. Sally had received back information about the outside world from those shippers returning from the shores of their trading partners. She had built up a mental encyclopedia of information and thanks to an excellent memory could answer most questions on the subject. Sally felt it was her responsibility to share some of the information she had received. However, some of the stories were interesting and some stories were horrific.

"I believe that our trading partner north of us, England, will be enjoying some similar celebrations. They have a sport which is played on horses. It requires the rider to strike a ball between two goal posts while riding their horse. The ball is much harder than the one used for our second racket game and the rider strikes it with what looks like a long wooden hammer."

"What about other parts of the world." Heather asked.

"English people are establishing colonies on the large continent west of Azorka." Sally said.

"England may help one of Azorka's oldest trading partners to modernize. Providing their intentions are good and they don't take advantage of them. Some of our trading partners living on this continent, have made their own agreements with the English settlers and other tribes further inland disagree and are suspicious of the settlers. But tonight, they will be resting from the hard work of building a settlement.'"

Sally wondered when she should tell Heather about more alarming events in the outside world. Like the blood drenched religious massacres that have been raging for the last eleven hundred years. The hideous persecution of those accused of witchcraft was an evil that persisted, often facilitating seizure of property belonging to the accused. The outside world was a mixed situation of disaster and slow progress towards modern living. That's why Azorka had agents all over the world to keep an eye on developing events.

Sally decided it would be best if she talked more about England, a trading partner with traditions that fascinated Heather.

"You remember that in England everyone has a last name. Well did you know that some of these people also have a title, like Duke or Duchess." Sally asked.

Heather was listening attentively; no one in Azorka had a last name so she was already intrigued with their trading partner's strange customs.

"The title gives them special recognition in their Royal Court and special duties to perform for the crown so that the people of England are well served. The result is a strengthened sense of pride on part of the titled individual and the motivation to perform their tasks with the greatest success." Sally finished. Sally got up from the table and took her empty plate to the kitchen sink. She took hold of her control console attached to her robe and aiming it at the kitchen window she pressed the button and the window slid into the recess cut into the kitchen wall. A fresh blast of morning air filled the kitchen.

"So, this beautiful morning I declare you are"Heather of Morning Dishes" and I'm expecting the cleanest dishes in the entire Kingdom." Sally said with a smile.

"Hey it's your turn to do the dishes. I did them yesterday." Heather replied.

While the two Princesses were arguing the kitchen duties, General Zen had reached the mountain home of the Zapatsaurs. He stood beside his Zapatsaur facing what must have been a committee of five Zapatsaurs. The third Zapatsaur moved forward with a stick clutched between its powerful hands. Then the Zapatsaur began sketching diagrams in the sand and five minutes later it stopped and returned to its position in line.

The General moved forward a little surprised by this Zapatsaurs ability to communicate so fluidly with diagrams. He looked down at a reasonable drawing of the Dragon Queen with a baby Zapatsaur gagged and clutched in her powerful arms. Two adult Zapatsaurs, he thought represented the parents, were in pursuit of the Dragon Queen in the evening air, the only time she would be out. The last diagram at first was confusing. It was an arrow after a drawing of land mass that resembled Azorka. Then it dawned on the General that the diagram was communicating the departure of the adult Zapatsaurs from Azorka heading in the direction of the Empire's island. This suggested that they were attempting a rescue of their child and that they could have met with a disastrous encounter with one of the Wizard's creatures which roam about the island at night. Quite possibly the Dragon Queen would deliver the baby to the Wizard and he would dissect the infant until he had all that he needed to create a smart creature. Azorka didn't want more cunning adversaries attacking its shores and maybe the rest of the outside world. And it didn't want the baby Zapatsaur to perish from the Wizard's evil experiment.

The General stepped back and addressed the five Zapatsaurs.

"For the next twenty-four hours I'm requesting that all of you who can avoid flight please do so until I have organized a suitable defense for your mountain home." He called out.

The General spoke loud enough that the entire Zapatsaur community would hear his voice echoing amongst the mountains, even though he knew they could read his thoughts.

"I also want you to know that we will be doing everything possible to rescue the baby Zapatsaur and its parents."

With that said, the General climbed back on to his Zapatsaur and set out for the Guardian's castle to report his findings to Sally.

She traveled in bright sunlight at one-hundred miles per hour, flying twenty-feet above the ocean surface. A hideous shadow danced on the choppy water below as the Dragon Queen raced towards Azorka. She had been traveling at full speed for the last hour and a half and finally her sharp eye sight could see the island in the distance. The Dragon Queen angled upwards sharply so that she could have a view of what was going on below. She knew the range of Azorka's best telescopes so she flew fast climbing to five thousand feet, where her eyes would still be sharp enough to see what was going on below while out of the eye shot of the military's observers.

She stopped above village 'C' and hovered in place. There wasn't a creature in the world, human or animal, that could see accurately at five-thousand feet. She looked down at General Zen as he mounted his Zapatsaur. He left the village flying in the direction of the Guardian's castle, probably to report what he had learned at the Zapatsaur's mountain home.

The Dragon Queen decided to follow him, knowing that she wouldn't be detected at this height. After twenty-minutes of traveling at top speed on his Zapatsaur, the General began his descent landing in the front yard of the megalith castle. He walked up to the hand carved front door and knocked. Heather answered and the General entered the castle while the Dragon Queen maintained her position hovering above, waiting for her opportunity to present itself.

Inside the castle, the General walked the long length of the hallway and into the kitchen with Heather. Sally had lost the argument over who would clean up the dishes and she was just finishing, the sleeves of her robe still rolled up. She looked up from her cleaning, surprised to see the General so soon.

"General you have some news already." She asked.

Sally could tell by the expression on the General's face that the news was not good.

"The Dragon Queen kidnapped a baby Zapatsaur and its parents left in pursuit chasing her in an attempt to rescue their child. They were probably flying full speed, at the same speed the Dragon Queen travels, until they reached the Empire's island." The General said.

The General's voice was flat with disappointment and Sally thought that he was feeling guilty for not having enough security posted in village 'C'. She was alarmed over this unexpected assault on the Zapatsaurs and was beginning to feel some of the Generals stress.

"What has happened to the three Zapatsaurs. Did they rescue the baby? Do we know the end result from their chase?" Sally asked.

Her voice was beginning to tremble. They had just spoken of this possibility not even twenty-four hours ago. This was her worst nightmare playing out early in the day.

"We haven't any news yet on the outcome of the pursuit. I'm going to send extra sentries armed with copper arrows to guard their mountain home. I've also asked the Zapatsaurs to restrict their movements and visibility, to refrain from flying until I can get security in place." The General answered.

"Thank you for acting quickly General. You must be shocked and alarmed as I am, although you hide your emotions well." Sally said. She didn't want the General blaming himself for the unexpected tragedy.

Heather was also shocked at hearing the news and she left Sally and the General in the kitchen to discuss the recent events. She moved to the backyard of the castle to check on the Zapatsaurs. Heather recognized her Zapatsaur from the purple flecks of color throughout its body and it was happily munching breakfast next to Sally's Zapatsaur. Suddenly it lifted its long neck and looked above as though somehow alarmed.

The Dragon Queen looked down at the two Zapatsaurs in the backyard, thinking that eventually the two ladies would move their meeting with the General to the outside patio. When the Zapatsaur raised its head, she could swear it was looking directly at her, even at five-thousand feet. Perhaps she had under estimated the abilities of these creatures. The Dragon Queen panicked and flew downwards to hover just above the trees which would hide her physically from the Zapatsaurs. Now it was just a case of letting her mind go blank to be assured that their telepathic abilities wouldn't be able to detect her presence. Hopefully, the Zapatsaurs wouldn't be able to locate her.

Heather was as protective of the Zapatsaurs as Sally. When she saw her Zapatsaur raise its head so suddenly she thought it had seen something in the sky so she opened the sliding glass door and stepped out to investigate. Heather looked up just in time to see the Dragon Queen swooping down on her. Then. everything went black and Heather lost consciousness as the Dragon Queen's enormous feet came in contact with her head. The Dragon Queen grasped both of Heather's shoulders with her powerful feet then rose into the sky quickly disappearing into a cloud which had, luckily for the Dragon Queen, been rolling by above.

Both Zapatsaurs abandoned their snack in the garden and were pacing back and forth anxiously. They began to make a piercing high-pitched sound like a cry or warning call which brought the General and Sally running to the backyard to see what was wrong. Sally looked upward into the morning sky just as the Dragon Queen left the cloud with her unconscious sister dangling from her monstrous feet.

CHAPTER 4

By the time Sally reached the back patio both Zapatsaurs were almost unable to contain their anxiety. Sally was already short tempered because of the recent tragedy within their community. But now the Dragon Queen had kidnapped her sister. She wanted to cut her to shreds so she grabbed her sword from the table in the hallway closest to the rear entrance. The Dragon Queen had a substantial lead, but Sally mounted her Zapatsaur and as soon as she was airborne began swinging her sword around and shouting out threats against the Dragon Queen. Sally had reached a height of about two hundred feet by the time the General arrived outside on the back patio. He had considered running around to the front yard to mount his own Zapatsaur but Heather's Zapatsaur seemed to be indicating by an odd mewling sound and lowering its neck that it would be happy to join the chase with the General as its rider. The General accepted the offer and soon they were in the morning sky about three-hundred yards behind Sally and narrowing the distance between them. After about twenty minutes of extreme exertion on the part of Heather's Zapatsaur, the General could see the Dragon Queen exiting a cloud with the unconscious Heather dangling from those monstrous feet. Sally reached into a pocket in her robe pulling out a laser derringer and began shooting at the Dragon Queen's wings once they were over the ocean. Sally was hoping that the Dragon Queen hadn't activated her force field. However, the Dragon Queen was very agile and evasive. She sped away from Sally at an incredible speed heading for a long patch of fog which had settled on the ocean surface. Sally stopped and hovered above the ocean waiting to see where the Dragon Queen would emerge. The General caught up and called out to Sally. "The fogs right across the ocean. It's better cover for her than the clouds were."

Sally looked back at the General and shouted out her reply against the roar of the wind.

"Let's head back and organize a small rescue party. Then we'll travel to the Empire's island and rescue Heather."

"That's a good idea. It will allow us to stock up on some necessary weapons and supplies. We will need to prepare a ship for the journey. The General shouted.

With that decision agreed upon they both turned back to the castle to prepare for the rescue. Sally was still raging with anger, but did her best to hide it.

Heather regained consciousness about one hour after her capture. The Dragon Queen had her shoulders in the powerful grip of her large feet and Heather was being carried along just about five-feet off the ocean surface through a heavy fog. Like the early morning clouds which concealed the first twenty minutes of the kidnapping, the patches of fog which peppered the ocean surface between the islands concealed the approach to the Empire's island. Heather's head hurt and her ears were stinging from the cold fog they were flying through at what must have been one-hundred miles per hour. The fog was leaving her robe damp and occasionally her feet were washed from the ocean spray. Hypothermia was becoming a very real concern.

Heather looked up at the Dragon Queen, her green face fixed in a grimace of hatred. The Dragon Queen was annoyed by the relentless chase. She had assumed the General would pursue her and had expected Sally to remain behind at their castle as the only guardian present in Azorka. Unfortunately, she was another hot-headed guardian to be dealt with. She flew after her in a fury brandishing her sword and shouting out threats. After twenty-five minutes Sally had almost caught up with her. Obviously her Zapatsaur had telepathically locked on to Heather. Then the Princess began taking"pot-shots" with her laser gun at her wings. This kind of challenge and anxiety taxed the Dragon Queen and she had not prepared for it. This left her no choice but to speed away faster or stop and engage her enemy. The Dragon Queen thought that she must have exceeded her top speed. She left Sally far behind disappearing into the layer of fog covering the surface of the ocean. She couldn't use her force field while carrying Heather due to the fact that it was designed for her body only and would detect the overlapping mass. So, she was still vulnerable until she dropped off her valuable package at the Wizard's castle. With this final thought she cleared the fog and as her good fortune would have it, she now faced home shore and a short distance away the Wizard's castle. Not a moment to soon as her energy level was depleted. She looked down at Heather her grimace now changed to an evil smile, her eyes charged with an unshakeable malevolence. Heather shrank from this sight and instead began moving her arms and hands over what parts of her body that she could reach in an effort to keep herself warm. In another ten minutes the Dragon Queen set Heather down in the castle's courtyard. The Dragon Queen's huge feet released Heather and she tumbled and rolled in the dust of the courtyard for about ten feet until coming to a stop. When she got up the Dragon Queen was standing still in front of her, wings retracted and waiting to lead Heather into the castle. A short grey figure appeared in the courtyard doorway leading into the wing with the reception room and laboratory. The Wizard smiled and called over to the Dragon Queen.

"Our guest has arrived! Splendid! I've been anxious to meet you Heather!" He called out in his deep voice.

The Wizard offered a pleasant smile as he faced Heather. He was about four feet tall his skin entirely grey and an average well trimmed beard, also grey, adorned a face with pudgy cheeks. But those black. eyes, penetrating and hypnotic made Heather fear the Wizard and heed all that had been said about him.

The Wizard waved them in from the doorway. Heather led the way stepping through the door into a hallway covered from ceiling to floor in a bright orange marble. Unlike the torches in the rear hallway and front turret staircase, which were wrapped in a flammable tar and left soot on the ceiling and wall, this hallway contained crystal powered candelabra built into the wall. Both the floor and walls gleamed and Heather could see her reflection as well as the disapproving expression on the face of the Dragon Queen directly behind her. At the end of the twenty-foot hallway the circular reception room was lit up by skylights above, specially installed within the mahogany covered ceiling. It was the same flexible glass that Azorka used for its domed roofs. This was a surviving technology common to both Kingdoms. Heather glanced behind in time to see the Dragon Queen remove her sunglasses and place them in a pocket of her white robe. The Wizard stood in the middle of the huge room patiently waiting for them. Heather walked into the same enormous reception room that Mitch and Tamara were in less than six hours ago. The luxurious furniture stood out elegantly in the late morning sun. The marble floor, now a more conservative blend of white and orange, held a reflection of the ceiling, a woodcarver's masterpiece, in places not covered by expensive area rugs. The decor conscious Wizard had created his own style in the reception room. Heather was wondering why she hadn't heard of his materialistic obsessions before.

The Dragon Queen entered the room behind Heather and the Wizard raised his arm in the direction of a wood paneled door in the back wall that joined the reception room to the larger complex and the laboratory. The Wizard pulled open the door and disappeared up a staircase with Heather and the Dragon Queen following. Heather was impressed with the dark rich mahogany walls of the staircase. There were twenty stairs, each one covered with a dark red carpet, but they still creaked a little as the silent procession made its way to the top landing. The Wizard was waiting at the end of a short twenty-foot hallway holding open the only door visible on this floor. Heather and the Dragon Queen entered a large seven-hundred square foot room decorated as lavishly as the downstairs reception room. This was the Wizards office and he walked over to his desk, circled its great width and opened his dark gold floor length drapes to reveal a large window behind that looked out in a north westerly direction at the ocean. The waves were heard crashing against the shoreline below, whipped up by a strong wind. The Wizard took his seat behind his desk.

In front of the desk was a large love seat elegant enough to be suitable furniture for any Royal Court in the outside world. Heather sat down on the comfortable love seat and faced the Wizard.

"Maria you look tired." The Wizard said, with an expression of sympathy washing over his face.

The Dragon Queen raised her black eye brows in surprise but said nothing. Heather was surprised to hear the Wizard call the Dragon Queen"Maria' but she also remained silent.

"Maria lay down on the couch and get some rest if you like." The Wizard offered. He pointed to his right where a large artistically upholstered couch hugged the mahogany paneled wall. But as inviting as it looked the Dragon Queen declined the offer and simply sat down in a chair on the opposite wall. Above the Dragon Queen were shelves of books and scrolls which circled the room. The Wizard's office looked more like a small library.

The Wizard relaxed in his chair like a teacher about to give a lesson to his students.

"Heather, I think the time has come when our Kingdoms have to consider working together. This useless competition or covert war must end." The Wizard began.

"There has always been this impression of conquering the outside world. That our Empire wants to rule the planet. Your perception of our motives could be incorrect Heather. We are acting out of self-defense from the inevitable. The outside world is becoming increasingly more violent. It's time to act in order to prevent disaster on this planet. They may cause a certain amount of damage to our atmosphere, food supply, the animal kingdom and the needless sufferings that on-going wars bring. This is why I asked Maria to bring you to me. We should discuss the possibility of becoming allies." The Wizard proposed. "What is it that you want with me!" Heather said. Her sharp reply was like an angry stab at the Wizard, revealing a strong distrust for his motives and it put him on the defensive.

The Wizard shifted in his chair looking a little uncomfortable.

"I apologize for your capture and less than comfortable journey here." The Wizard said.

He looked over at the Dragon Queen who was sitting as motionless as a reptile. Her expression was blank and he could see that she could not care less whether or not Heather was in any discomfort.

"But I hope to make it up to you by having you stay here as my most valued guest." The Wizard said with his most sincere smile.

Heather slowly raised her eyebrows in a gesture that suggested she was not convinced of his sincerity.

"I'm sure you'll find the accommodations in the back tower comfortable." The Wizard said.

"Again! What is it you want from me!" Heather yelled.

The Wizard's expression changed his dark eyes flared up in anger and he shouted back at Heather.

"One! I need to educate you on our intentions and what we have found about the outside world which is alarming. Two! I need you to participate in a harmless experiment. Three! I need your silence about our two Kingdoms as I have another guest residing in the tower who is from the outside world." The Wizard shouted.

Heather was not impressed nor was she intimidated by the Wizard's showmanship and shot back at him.

"You have a guest from the outside world!" Heather said, her eyes wide in an expression of amazement."Do you know how overwhelmed our two Kingdoms would be if we were discovered. The lives it would cost as a result of invasion should be sufficient reason to abandon any thoughts about communicating with the outside world at this point in their development. At least until they have peacefully evolved and civilized. This has always been Azorka's policy and any effort to interrupt the outside world's natural progression will not be tolerated."

"Heather the outside world is becoming increasingly more violent." The Wizard explained in a calmer voice.

"Countries are going to war against each other over cultural differences and land disputes. They cannot settle their affairs peacefully. They need the guidance our civilizations can provide." The Wizard said.

"I don't agree with a forceful solution and I know that Azorka won't either. Your proposal for an alliance would be rejected." Heather calmly stated.

If it was natural for the Wizard's complexion to flash red, he certainly would have out of anger and frustration. He just sat there in a moment of silence then spoke quietly.

"The outside world doesn't have the civility to create committees to oversee their disputes and bring to the table a peaceful solution. We need to join forces, overwhelm their military, then dictate the terms for their peaceful resolutions." The Wizard said.

"That sort of forced control is not going to work Wizard!" Heather shouted.

"Azorka has agents throughout the outside world reporting weekly on events taking place. We are not in the dark or ignorant of what is going on. What you propose is an invasion which will cost lives because it's human nature to resist." Heather finished.

It was obvious to the Wizard that he would get nowhere in this discussion with Heather. Maybe the oldest Guardian of Azorka would be the wisest. He decided to drop the subject altogether.

Heather remained silent. She just stared at the Wizard with a look of disgust.

The Wizard got up from his desk and walked over to a shelve just above the Dragon Queen's head. He pointed up at a dark blue object resting on the shelf. Then he reached up, stretching his four-foot frame to its maximum and brought it down from its resting place. He walked back over to his desk, grasping the top halve of the object and setting it down facing Heather. It was a dark blue human skull crafted from quartz.

"What you are looking at now, that is when you're not looking daggers at me, is my property from over ten-thousand years ago. When the war between our Kingdoms was moving towards an end, someone broke into my laboratory and stole this from me. The thieves were also able to locate the other twelve crystal skulls and steal them as well. I need to have them back. I just happened to find this one in the possession of the outsider that you will meet later. I actually rescued him from a turbulent ocean that would otherwise have drowned him. He was the Captain of a pirate ship which had been out-gunned and destroyed by the Portuguese navy. This is the trading partner Azorka pays taxes to in order to live and trade from the largest of the islands in the Azores. This pirate, the only survivor, was clinging to a large board which had been blown off the doomed ship. He wouldn't let go of a small chest which contained some precious jewels and my crystal skull. I had Maria rescue him and by the time she reached him floating in the water he had passed out but miraculously still had the chest clutched in his arms. So fortunately, all I had to do was keep Maria and my creatures out of sight and I could explain myself as a well to do magician living alone on an undesirable island." The Wizard explained.

Heather didn't have a question for him. The Wizard continued with his speech.

"I would like you to tell my guest that you are my niece. I'm sure I can count on your cooperation. For now, I would like you to get some rest so that you will recover from today's ordeal. Maria will show you to your living quarters in the tower where you'll find a meal of smoked grouse and fresh fruit waiting for you. I have also included some reading material for you on modern agricultural methods you might find interesting." The Wizard offered.

The silence in the room marked the end of the meeting and the Dragon Queen got up from her chair and walked out of the Wizard's office with Heather following behind. They retraced their steps through the castle till they were outside in a bright early afternoon sun. Heather looked at the Dragon Queen who had just put on her sunglasses.

"So, your real name is Maria." She asked.

"Yes. Just over ten-thousand years ago I volunteered for the Wizard's experiment which had military applications. The experiment, if it had worked, would grant the subject the ability to manipulate their own body mass. The subject in reality, would be biologically changed so that he or she would become a shape-shifter. Before the experiment began, I had to choose the shape I would shift to and then this was programmed into the experiment. During the war as you know there were many casualties and I lost my entire family to an aerial strike orchestrated by the Aryans in Azorka. No one in the Empire could design. flying machines that were reliable. The Aryans produced flying machines so efficient and reliable that when war broke out Azorka took advantage of their expertise and used it to deliver deadly strikes against the Empire. At this time the Wizard's flying creatures were deadlier than they are now but they were challenged by the Aryan's air force." The Dragon Queen finished.

"You did destroy the Aryan air force and their only factory, located close to our southern beach, along with the technology now lost. But I guess I can't blame you for wanting revenge if you lost your family." Heather said.

The Dragon Queen was thinking that Heather had softened up a little and was wondering if she would slip up in conversation and provide her with information about Azorka.

"Yes Heather, their air force delivered the killing blow with the Firestone, which caused two-hundred miles of civilization to sink to the bottom of the ocean. Then the Aryan's only remaining aircraft crashed on the way back to home base and their technology was completely lost. Half of your land and half our land contained the most advanced technology on the planet." The Dragon Queen said.

By this time, they had left the courtyard by the front entrance and were walking around to the backyard. where the tower, thirty yards away, was located.

"For five-thousand years Azorka had no means of flight until the Zapatsaur mysteriously appeared. What do you think they did with the Firestone."? The Dragon Queen asked.

"I don't know Maria. That is one of Azorka's most guarded secrets." Heather replied.

The Dragon Queen had figured as much but Heather was in a weakened state and could have slipped up. She had to ask. The Dragon Queen's best guess was the bank but she wasn't sure of that, she also wasn't sure of its appearance or size. If she could just break in to the Azorkan bank she could confirm whether or not the Firestone was there. If not, she could consider other possibilities. Stealing the Firestone would be like a short cut to world domination.

"Yes of course. I should have realized its location would be a shared secret amongst the select few." The Dragon Queen returned.

They both arrived at the tower the Wizard used to house his guests. It was artistically crafted inside with a gilded bannister for the circular staircase. The fieldstone walls of the outside continued on the inside. The domed ceiling at the top of the staircase, was painted with a hunting scene that seemed to be a representation of the culture and countryside in a European country. The hunters were strangely dressed in red and black, and the painted houses in the background had wooden shingles on peaked roofs with chimneys.

They reached the top level and the Dragon Queen stopped in front of Heather's room.

"This is your room on the right here." She said.

The Dragon Queen opened the door for Heather.

"Tomorrow you'll meet our guest from the outside world. Right now, he is tending to his ship a slight distance from here in a small cove. The Wizard believes this location hides his new ships from competitors. It could also be mistaken as a pirate vessel and the world governments are sworn to hunt down and destroy piracy. That's why I'm able to move about secure in the knowledge he won't spot me."

"We have removed just about all the creatures to the network of tunnels below so they're out of sight during the daytime. All this trouble so he won't find out about our advanced civilizations."

"By the way he's the one responsible for getting all the furniture and handwoven rugs you see that are suitable for royalty, from the outside world. This pirate I rescued about a year ago is more like an employee for the Wizard. The Wizard will be sending him out on various missions. So, I'll be spending most of my time in the comfort of my cave until he leaves." The Dragon Queen finished.

"I'm to introduce myself as the Wizard's niece. Don't worry we have a mutual interest." Heather assured the Dragon Queen.

With that being said, the Dragon Queen abruptly turned and descended the stairs leaving Heather to take in her surroundings. She shut the door and could see that her small apartment was in the shape of a wedge of cheese with the back wall and window, its widest point and rounded to match the shape of the tower. It was well furnished with the same European furniture that was featured throughout the castle. The bed had been expertly hand-carved and the bedcover decorated with an intricate pattern of orange and red paisleys. Her small desk was a dark wood polished so well she could see her reflection. On the desktop a small meal of smoked grouse and fruit was waiting as the Wizard had promised. Beside the desk a small book case containing literature on modern farming was waiting to be read.

Heather walked over to her window and opened it just in time to see the Dragon Queen flying by and chasing three pheasants flapping their wings as fast as they could in order to escape her. Heather watched as the Dragon Queen caught all three wild birds with the lightning speed of a reptile and wrung their necks for a quick and merciful end. She had an exquisite meal planned now that she had the pheasants.

Heather turned away from the window and walked to the center of the room and sat down on a loveseat very much like the one in the Wizard's office. It was expertly upholstered and very comfortable but before sleep became a temptation, she reached inside her robe pocket and brought out the control console she used at home to open doors and windows and the various other entrances in Azorka.

Heather was thinking back to an enjoyable dinner date she had with her boyfriend 'Ted". He had suggested they enjoy a pheasant and cooked vegetable dinner at a small eatery the military sometimes frequented. It was a delicious dinner and they had tea afterwards, which is when Ted, who was a young officer in the military, told her about the breakthrough in crystal technology. The Azorkan research center had developed a homing device that would locate the target should they be lost or captured. It was a silent device that sent out a pulsating sensation to the person wearing the belt. The pulsometer was sewn into the center of the belt. Ted told Heather he had permission to install it in her control console if she would like to participate in the experiment. Ted was always worried about Heather. Since their school days together he had thought Heather would be kidnapped some day because she would fetch a handsome ransom for the Empire. Heather thought he was over protective but agreed to the experiment so Ted installed the signal chip in her control console. That same evening Ted had flown back to the castle with Heather. After a short while a military messenger had flown to the castle to tell Ted he was urgently needed. He handed the belt to Heather to keep for the following evening when he would return and they could try it out together. Heather had put it around her Zapatsaur's neck for safe keeping. But Ted was called away on duty longer than he had anticipated and Heather hasn't seen him since that night.

Heather looked at the switch Ted had installed on her control console. The Wizard said he had quarantined all his creatures. The Dragon Queen had retired to her cave until the visitor has gone out on another mission for the Wizard. But she still felt that if she activated the device it would put her Zapatsaur in danger. Heather knew her Zapatsaur would come to her rescue. The Zapatsaur would have read both Ted's and her thoughts on that last night they were together. Her beautiful creature would risk its own life for Heather. She decided not to activate the switch. She put her control console back in her robe pocket and sat back enjoying the comfort of the loveseat.

She began to drift in thought. Heather was tired but she began to wonder why the Wizard had bothered to show her the crystal skull. She couldn't care less about his lost property. Did he think that someone in Azorka stole the other twelve crystal skulls?

Perhaps the Wizard was watching my expression for recognition. Did he think I'd say that Azorka has one or two just like it?

Heather abandoned this line of thought and reached for one of the Wizard's manuals on modern agriculture to simmer down her racing thoughts. In the morning she would figure out how to escape the island. She eventually drifted off to sleep as the sun began its daily descent.

CHAPTER 5

Sally and the General had arrived back at the castle about forty-minutes before Heather had gone into the Wizard's office. Heather's Zapatsaur had left them after a short rest and had returned to its mountain home. Sally had invited the General in for a warm cup of tea. She had recovered from her rage and anger and spoke with the General in a more controlled and professional manner. The General was impressed with Sally's professional façade, and her ability to gain control over the situation. He knew she was concerned for her sister and feeling responsible for not ordering the capture of the Dragon Queen. Even the General couldn't believe the Dragon Queen's tenacity and vicious behavior; from what he'd seen Heather might be suffering from a concussion. The General assured Sally that her earlier decisions were well thought out. If they had captured the Dragon Queen, the Wizard would have organized a rescue and in the process would have stumbled in to Mitch and Tamara's covert mission. Sally thanked him for his good words, then let him know that they must now rescue Heather and capture the Dragon Queen. Some great military planning began.

Sally believed that with the kidnapping, new considerations were on the table and that preparations for a rescue of Heather and capture of the Dragon Queen was good organization. Sally asked the General to have his men prepare her ship which was outfitted for military missions. She also asked him to pack the specially developed copper arrow he had mentioned would render the Dragon Queen unconscious. They would set sail in the morning with the General's own handpicked crew and two Zapatsaurs which would be hidden in the ship's hold. The General and Sally were organized for Heather's rescue.

The General left Sally shortly after to make the preparations they had discussed for Heather's rescue. Presently, Sally was watching the sun set in the west through a clearing in the forest, on the back patio. She was relaxing and planning the mission further, trying to anticipate the unexpected which might threaten the mission's success. She was also considering a ransom of cooperation delivered to the Wizard once they had the Dragon Queen secured in chains. But the rescue of her sister was her greatest concern.

The Wizard would be tempted to subject Heather to coercive questioning in order to extract information about Azorka, Sally wanted the swift rescue of Heather in order to spare her this tortuous experience. A wave of anxiety temporarily washed over her. She wished that the King and Queen were back so she could check her military plan with greater expertise. Fifteen-minutes later Sally's wish was granted. A messenger arrived and announced the arrival of Mitch and Tamara. The ship had docked on Azorka's southern shore and they were on their way to the castle. They had arrived early from their mission. One hour later Mitch and Tamara arrived home at the castle. Their Zapatsaurs departed almost immediately with the baby Zapatsaur riding on the back of Tamara's Zapatsaur. It was likely they were returning to their mountain home to give an account of the tragedy which caused the deaths of the baby Zapatsaurs parents. Their telepathy was restricted to distance, though no one knew the maximum distance that they could communicate from, it was generally assumed to be fifty miles because of the proximity of village C.

Mitch removed his coat and Tamara fumbled in her pocket for her control console. She opened the front door and they both walked down the long hallway to the kitchen where the only light in the castle was on. Sally looked up from the kitchen table as Mitch and Tamara walked in the room.

"Mom and Dad, it is so good to see you! How did the mission go?" She asked.

Sally had prepared herself and worked out a brief explanation for Heather's abduction. She knew with the news blackout and secrecy that must be maintained to avoid panic, that the King and Queen would not be aware of the kidnap.

Mitch was looking forward to a little rest and he smiled as he looked around the kitchen and spoke at the same time. He was really hungry for some grouse or pheasant pie.

"Our mission was successful and we rescued the baby Zapatsaur the Dragon Queen had kidnapped. Unfortunately, the baby's parents were destroyed by one of the Wizard's creatures."

Mitch had stopped smiling as he remembered this tragic part of their mission. The news hit Sally like a ton of bricks but she hid her feelings and began to give an account of events that had taken place while they were gone.

"Yesterday morning I received a report concerning the Dragon Queen. She had invaded Azorka and attacked two of our guards at the bank. She tried to laser the bank's door open but a military squad on duty caught her in the act. The squad were able to describe the laser gun. They fired a copper arrow at her which scared her away so fast they were unsure as to which direction she flew. I summoned General Zen to discuss the incident and asked him to check the Zapatsaurs mountain home the next morning to see if the Dragon Queen had disrupted their community. He arrived back this morning and told me about the kidnap and pursuit by two Zapatsaurs, the baby's parents. This was communicated to him by diagrams drawn by the Zapatsaur's, he assumed, appointed official." Sally said in her calm tone of voice. She looked at her parents and wondered how they would react to the kidnap of Heather.

"This morning, Heather was kidnapped by the Dragon Queen while she was checking on the Zapatsaurs in the backyard. The Zapatsaurs were acting strangely and looking up into the sky. Heather must have looked up just as the Dragon Queen was swooping down on her. It would seem the Dragon Queen knocked her unconscious. By the time I reached the patio I looked up and saw my unconscious sister exiting a cloud, dangling from the feet of the Dragon Queen." Sally said.

Sally felt awful for Mitch and Tamara having to deal with this new problem after returning from a difficult rescue. She went on to explain yesterday's decision and why she decided not to order the capture of the Dragon Queen for the assault on the bank guards. Instead she had asked the General to observe the movements of the Dragon Queen, which would provide a small margin of safety and not disrupt her parents mission.

Mitch was first to speak."Your decisions were good. General Zen would have to travel all the way to the Empire's island in order to capture the Dragon Queen and his presence would be obvious. It would have sent warning signals out to the Wizard. He would have posted extra sentries and spoiled our mission by making it more difficult to rescue the baby Zapatsaur."

Tamara walked over to the marble kitchen table and sat down across from Sally. She smiled with approval of her oldest daughter's performance while in charge of Azorka.

"You did your best and both your father and I are proud. I'm glad you're prepared to set out in the morning for the rescue."

Sally went on to explain the General's new development from the Azorkan Research Department; the copper arrow which would cause the Dragon Queen to lose consciousness. It was Sally's decision to finally capture her and put her in chains. The General helped her organize a military assault on the Empire and would assist with the capture of the Dragon Queen.

"That's good organization during the very stressful moments you experienced. You should realize though that the Dragon Queen is very dangerous. Next time let General Zen chase her because he is experienced. I know you are one of the champion swords-women in

Azorka but don't let that cloud your judgement. Both the Wizard and the Dragon Queen are very dangerous." Tamara advised.

Mitch spoke up after Tamara had finished. He wanted Tamara to rest up at home and keep a look out for any kind of counter invasion by the Wizard. There was no guarantee that the arrow would work because it hadn't been tested. Still he thought this worth a try and was glad about Sally's swift decision to try it.

"Your ship will be ready in the morning so I'll travel along with you and the General. There is enough room in the cargo hold for my Zapatsaur. I'll need Tamara to stay in Azorka in order to prepare Azorka for any kind of surprise attack which may result." Mitch finished.

Tamara nodded her head in approval.

"Heather is tough as nails. I know she will be fine till we rescue her." Tamara said.

Tamara's reassurance was soothing and Sally looked up from the kitchen table and smiled with relief."Dad and I will get the Dragon Queen. We'll use her to get the cooperation we want from the Wizard."

Mitch considered the possibility of any cooperation by the Wizard to be heavily laced with deceit and trickery. Right now, he was willing to agree just to settle down Sally so that she'd get a good rest tonight. He looked across the table at Tamara and from the expression on her face she must have been thinking the same thing.

"That's an excellent plan Sally but we have to get some rest. The next twenty-four hours are going to be busy and challenging." Mitch said.

"You are going to need all your rest to be focused and prepared for the expected and the unexpected challenges." Tamara said.

Sally knew her parent's advice was good. She wanted to be at her best to accomplish everything necessary for her planned invasion to be a success.

"You're absolutely right about the importance of being well rested and focused for the task at hand. I'll be fresh to go in the morning." Sally replied.

Mitch looked down at his daughter and smiled. She had grown into a courageous twenty-four-year-old woman he was very proud of, but she would always be his little girl. He shifted from leaning against the wall and sat down at the table with the ladies.

"How about I tell you that old bedtime story about how the Zapatsaurs were first discovered in Azorka." He said.

Sally gave her Mom a quick glance rolling her eyes in a polite mockery of her Father's offer. Tamaral acknowledged her gesture with a quick smile. Mitch had missed the silent communication between Mother and Daughter and began with the story.

"It was about five-thousand years ago and our fishermen were making their way home to village E on the west coast fifteen-miles south of village C. They had enjoyed a successful catch that day. The fishermen arrived at their secret entrance, ready to navigate through a circuitous and rocky ten-mile route to dock, a path no other mariner would consider navigating. Just before setting out on the ten-mile route, they noticed huge numbers of dolphins poking their heads above the surface of the ocean and calling out to a peculiar looking group of fourteen-foot long flying lizards that were feeding them fish. They were hovering above the ocean, entirely grey in color with three-digit feet and hands which would drop a fish into the mouth of a dolphin when it broke the surface. It was like a game for the Zapatsaurs and the dolphins. The Zapatsaur would dive into the ocean then come up with at least three fish to give to the dolphins. The fishermen were amazed at the sight of this new creature. It could fly and swim under water.

The flying creatures, they thought there were ten that day, seemed peaceful and playful."

"Unfortunately, after an hour of fun the school of fish below eventually left and the Zapatsaurs were saddened by the sudden change putting a quick end to their game. So, our fishermen called out to the Zapatsaurs donating their huge catch to the game and the Zapatsaurs and dolphins continued to have fun for the next three hours. On that day Azorkans and Zapatsaurs entered into a never ending and inspirational relationship." Mitch finished.

"Thank you, Dad. That's a bedtime story I've always enjoyed hearing." Sally said. "I think I shall get some sleep now. Good night."

Sally smiled to herself as she left the kitchen and walked down the long hallway, and through the living room which would take her to a beautifully gold gilded staircase. She'd climb twenty stairs to the top landing and walk twenty-feet down to her bedroom where she would happily collapse into a deep sleep.

Mitch looked across the table at Tamara. He noticed a different expression on her features now that Sally had left the room.

"Everything is going to be fine. I'll rescue Heather and we'll capture the Dragon Queen. Sally and I will be home from our mission in about two days or sooner." He said.

They both got up from the table and Tamara hugged Mitch.

"After you leave in the morning I'll organize extra security for the Zapatsaurs and the castle grounds. Right now, I am going to follow my daughter's lead and get some rest. I know I can count on you both to rescue Heather." She said.

Tamara walked out of the kitchen and traced the same path Sally had taken five minutes earlier in order to reach her bedroom and collapse into a deep sleep. Mitch decided to take a chair in the living room where he could view the front yard through the large recessed window. He'd be ready in case of an attack by the Dragon Queen before they set out. But he had overestimated his stamina and was fast asleep in no time.

While the Guardians of Azorka slept, the Wizard had decided to make the half mile journey to the cove. Leif the Lion was the pirate he had rescued on that fateful night. He had lost his ship and all his crew. The Wizard had set up a ship building bay inside a large cave with a high ceiling that faced the cove. He had supplied a crew of ten of his most reliable day time military sentries whose eyes were not as sensitive to the sunlight as the other residents who spent most of their time underground. They helped build the new ship for Leif, which was average in size with twenty cannons, six sails to catch the wind, and a comfortable Captain's quarters. One of the sentries had a talent for woodwork and he had carved a lion's head and placed it on the port side of the stern, just below the Captain's window, much to Leif's delight. Sam, the talented woodcarver, was a senior sentry of average height, about five-foot eight, with short grey hair surrounding a large bald spot. He was a little bit stout with a pot belly, sometimes clean shaven, and had a jolly personality. Leif was looking forward to the journey with Sam as his positive nature would serve the mission well during challenging moments.

The crew were putting the finishing touches on the ship by moonlight. So, Leif decided he would return to the castle for some rest. He was walking down the dock towards the same trail the Wizard was approaching on. He casually wiped perspiration from his forehead and ran his hand through his dark unkept hair. Leif didn't have a beard or mustache and was never clean shaven. His pale complexion lit up in the moonlight and the Wizard watched him walking towards him. Leif's blue shirt and grey pants were dirty but he had the look of satisfaction pasted to his features, and after several days of hard work he was pleased, as any pirate would be, with the results.

Leif reached the end of the dock and heard the crunch of a small branch underfoot just ahead of him. He instinctively looked up to see the smiling face of his grey skinned, four-foot tall host standing in the moonlight.

"Wizard it's good to see you and you'll be pleased to know that we'll be ready to sail tomorrow. I've had all the supplies loaded on the ship. We're ready to get the second crystal skull that Monsieur Lobau told me about. If we have clear sailing weather, Haiti will be a short journey from here." He said.

The Wizard was smiling and pleased with the progress of Leif and the crew.

"I am sending an additional ship and another ten crew members with you. Sam will be the Captain of the second ship." He said.

The Wizard had confidence in Sam's abilities and leadership. He could trust him to discreetly use the laser weapons without Leif being aware.

The Empire's ship was often used for missions into the outside world. If challenged by pirates, those unfortunate souls would find them themselves in the water and their skull and bones ship sinking to the depths of the ocean. Cannon fire from enemy ships at a distance, would not be able to penetrate a force field surrounding the ship. After briefly shutting down the force field, a laser cannon which was disguised as a traditional cannon was fired at the invaders then the force field would be turned back on to protect the ship. Unfortunately, the force field wouldn't work reliably if people were boarding the Empire's ship as it would detect the extra mass and automatically shut down.

The Wizard made a mental note to remind Sam and his crew of this safety feature in his briefing with them. The Wizard would be careful to explain to those involved in the mission that every precaution must be taken so that Leif would not witness the laser weapons in use or any other advanced technology that would be difficult to explain. The Empire's existence must be kept secret until they are ready to dictate terms to the world.

"I also wanted you to know that my niece is visiting me and staying across the hall from you. Please keep our activities secret and avoid discussion with her. Go back to the tower now and get some rest. I had my lady servant prepare a small meal for you and it's waiting in your room. I am very pleased with what I see. You are going to be a rich man Leif." The Wizard said.

Leif gave a nod of his head and walked past the Wizard and up the trail. The Wizard moved down the dock to brief Sam and the crew.

The next day, morning arrived cloudy and windy. Heather had woken up in the middle of the night on the loveseat with the Wizard's book in her lap. She thought a door slammed somewhere in the tower but didn't bother to investigate. Instead she got up and took off her shirt and pants which were still damp and spread them out on a chair to dry then went back to sleep on the bed. Eight hours later she was glad she did. Her clothes were dry and she was well rested. The Wizard knocked on her door just as she finished dressing. Heather opened the door to a jolly and smiling Wizard.

"Well I think we'll have fun today Heather. But first let's get a good breakfast into you. I've had my lady servant cook you a meal fit for a Queen. Eggs wrapped with a thin slice of grouse and pheasant as the main course. It will all simply melt in your mouth and dessert includes chocolate pudding and some of our island pears in cream and maple syrup." The Wizard said.

Heather couldn't help but smile because he looked so comical.

"Lead the way Wizard." She said.

They both went down the steps of the tower and through the back hall that Tamara and Mitch had used. Breakfast was arranged in the reception room close to the kitchen entrance. A round oak table large enough to seat four was set up with silver cutlery and decorative plates. The main dishes occupied the extra area at the table and were on fancy silver stands with a candle burning underneath to keep the pheasant and eggs warm. Heather sat down and waited until the Wizard was seated before starting into. her breakfast. The Wizard was gracious and polite. He passed the dishes to his guest before serving himself. They ate in silence for fifteen minutes then dessert arrived. After the chocolate pudding and the pears in maple syrup had been consumed the Wizard looked up meeting Heather's eyes which in his opinion were registering satisfaction. He felt it was a good time to begin his talk.

"You know Heather our ancestors lived in a slightly different world than we do today. There was a time, as you know, when this was all one land and we were working together. Of course, we gradually drifted apart because of slightly different viewpoints. But before that we held the most advanced technology in the world. Your ancestors saw those days and knew their way around those laboratories and complexes. Now they are at the bottom of the ocean but our machinery is still very usable as the material our advanced devices are made with are not subject to rust." The Wizard paused. It looked like he was resisting the urge to burp.

The Wizard recovered from his urge to belch and carried on.

"We can't recover them yet because we haven't developed our submersibles to withstand the underwater pressures of the ocean. If we can locate approximately where on the ocean floor they are resting and how deep, calculating the ocean pressure will be easier, more accurate. I propose today that we seek the location of the Aryan's factories. They were, at the time, expert builders of those submersibles. This will benefit Azorka because their factories were located very close to your southern shoreline. You can take home this information and my message which is a willingness to work out a truce between our two Kingdoms." The Wizard finished.

Heather was suspicious of this offer. It could be a deception. She was interested in knowing how the Wizard would accomplish this. He said that he intended to release her so she could take home this offer of peace. Heather felt it her duty to cooperate as a truce could be beneficial for both Kingdoms. She decided to take a chance that he was telling the truth.

"How can I help locate these factories?" She asked.

"Follow me up to my office and I'll show you some technology that survived the war." The Wizard said. They both rose from the table and climbed the stairs to the Wizard's office. Heather took her seat in front of the desk and the Wizard opened its bottom drawer and removed what looked like a salad bowl with a strap connected to it. He held it out for Heather to see. She took the object which was actually made of a polished metal and saw that the brown leather strap was fused into the object. She could see that it was designed to fit on a subject's head, most likely hers. The inside was rippled with indentations that went all around the inside of the object in various and random directions. Heather placed it on her head. She found it light and comfortable.

"I take it you want me to wear this Wizard. How will this help us locate the Aryan's factory?" Heather asked.

The Wizard was glad she asked this question.

"Let me explain. First of all, this is technology interpreting the human brain's memory functions from generation to generation. Its purpose is to unlock those memories from the unconscious and transfer them to the conscious, so we can examine them. Each one of those indentations inside my medical helmet has been carved out to match the location of specific regions of your brain. The outside surface is a finely polished metal. On the face of the helmet is a three-square inch crystal which is not visible to the naked eye. We called it Photonic crystal before the war and it collects the information from the helmet. This type of crystal is extremely sensitive and can be relied upon, in this application, for the accurate transfer of your thoughts into this screen on the table. So, it is like a high-tech artist converting your thoughts into images transferred to a screen, like a high-tech canvas." The Wizard explained.

The Wizard pointed to a ten by twelve-inch screen sitting upright on a stand on a small table three feet from Heather to her right.

"The screen is a receiver and display of what you are thinking. It is a graphic marvel." The Wizard said.

"So, the sender is built into my helmet. Is this safe to use. Is it going to hurt me or affect my health."? Heather asked.

"There will be no sensation or pain. If anything, it will be a relaxing experience for you." The Wizard said."How is it going to help us locate the lost factory?" Heather asked.

"Everyone has what is called a genetic memory. This is all of the collective experiences your ancestors remembered in their lifetime. These memories are inherited at birth. Some people can go through their lifetime and not use this information. Sometimes they can react to events or conditions like war or night time subconsciously, by being uncomfortable from night time traveling or instinctively becoming combat efficient during war. The reaction in this case would be fear because their ancestors would have experienced these conditions or events. The same can be said for happy events like understanding how to be an effective fisherman. People call this instinct but it is actually a subconscious how-to-do memory which has been passed down.

"The helmet extracts those memories through suggestion or vocal prompting. For example, I ask you a question which is vocal prompting. You think about my question and answer it from your memory. The result shows up on the other side of the screen. You won't see the results but I will. This way we can locate the factory because your ancestor was there for the tour when she was a Guardian. You have that memory buried inside your subconscious. The experiment will be easy to conduct because we know the time frame and I already knew the Guardian you are related to. You know I have a long life-span." The Wizard explained.

Heather said nothing about his life-span comment, assuming this to be an Azorkan secret that she will learn more about when she turns twenty-five. The rest of the information she examined. It would be advantageous to have the flying machines back and operating for Azorka. This in itself was a peace offering. The lost factory belonged to her Kingdom and the Wizard was actually helping Azorka to gain an advantage. He couldn't possibly be interested in continuing the war.

"Let's begin Wizard." Heather said.

"When I said this would be a relaxing experience I was sincere. In our Kingdom during the war our medical doctors could calm an individual through what we call hypnotism. It was useful for dealing with war fright." The Wizard said.

He opened a top drawer in his desk and took out a round piece of crystal about one inch in circumference.

"I need you to concentrate on this crystal and listen to my voice and do as I say. The idea is for you to become relaxed and comfortable then answer my questions" He said.

The Wizard moved a chair in front of Heather so that he was no more than three feet away and sat down. He held up the crystal and began swinging it side to side by its short chain. It moved back and forth like a pendulum swinging slowly in front of Heather as her eyes gradually became glazed over."Now I want you to relax and count backwards from one-hundred." The Wizard said.

Heather began counting."Ninety-nine, ninety-eight, ninety-seven," She said in a voice that seemed disconnected with the present,'sounding far away'.

"That's good Heather. Now while you are counting I want you to think back about everything you know about your Kingdom's past." The Wizard gently prompted.

Heather was still counting."Seventy-five, seventy-four, seventy-three." She continued.

"Now you will be going back in time five hundred years for every number that you count. When you sense that you've counted backwards to an ancestor who was a Guardian for Azorka than I want you to stop and tell me what you see." The Wizard instructed.

Heather was listening to the Wizard and counting backwards at the same time.

"Fifty-two, fifty-one, fifty."

Then suddenly she stopped. Her eyes were still staring into some unknown place unblinking and she had a blank expression on her face. She stared through the Wizard like he wasn't seated in front of her.

"Now what is the approximate date or year in Azorka where you are now. What is the name of your ancestor who is the Guardian." The Wizard prompted.

Heather opened her eyes wider like she was seeing something then she replied in her monotone voice.

"It is five years before the big war. My ancestor is Julia, a Guardian who is in charge of factory inspections." Heather said.

This was perfection the Wizard thought. The records show the Guardian that inspected the second Firestone on Empire territory, was Julia.

This Firestone was developed after the completion of the Firestone in the north, now hidden in Azorka. The Wizard like the Dragon Queen was not sure where it was hidden today. The Firestone was crafted as a power source that would sit at the top of a pyramid gathering energy from the sun and sending that energy back out of the pyramid and along the Earth's magnetic ley lines. Pyramids were placed on the connecting ley lines by those communities receiving energy, in this case the southern part of Azorka. The Guardians of Azorka wanted to work quickly towards world unity using free energy, a diplomatic carrot, as a benefit for all. However, the faction of rebels in the south wanted to tax and control those same countries in return for the energy. This led to the conflict which saw the conversion of the Firestone into a weapon for both sides. The location of the second Firestone was kept secret before its transfer to the pyramid. The Wizard at the time, secretly a rebel, was working on his creatures in a huge underground facility so he was not aware of the location. The other rebels who were participating in the Firestone espionage had been killed off during the final days of the war. The espionage was the conversion of the peaceful energy source into a weapon, and these rebels had perfected their art of concealment, so they thought. This is why he required Heather's assistance and participation in the experiment. He had no intention of locating the Aryan's factory and he would give her a phony location to take back to Azorka. When the experiment was complete he would be able to calculate the ocean pressures so he could begin the recovery of the Empire's Firestone.

The Wizard got up from his chair and walked over to the screen receiving images of what Heather was seeing in her hypnotized state.

"Heather what day is it and where is Julia going." The Wizard asked.

The Wizard could see Julia on the screen. She was a little taller than Heather and had jet black hair that fell to her shoulders. She was dressed in a white robe and was being accompanied with other officials on an Aryan flying machine. The Wizard recognized the buildings they flew over on the screen. They were on their way to southern Azorka. The flying machine was shaped like a tube with glass covering the upper half and polished metal below. It was outfitted with several chairs and the occupants were safely strapped in for high speed travel, sometimes as fast as seven-hundred miles per hour. The flying machines bottom portion was outfitted with a series of working flaps recessed into its smooth metallic body. The Ayrans were always vague about their flying machines, so it was believed that it was powered by crystal technology.

The Wizard could see it now flying next to some familiar counselor homes and offices. Julia must be getting close to the secret facility.

Heather still sounded far away with her monotone voice, when she answered the Wizard.

"Julia is inspecting a secret facility in the south on a Monday morning. She is thinking what a beautiful day in July. She is also thinking about her task ahead which is to document all of the machinery and tools used to craft the Firestone." Heather replied.

The Wizard smiled as he knew that the facility would remain the permanent facility for Firestone inspections. Then it would be transferred back to the pyramid built on the magnetic ley lines to serve as south Azorka's power source. Routine maintenance and monitoring of its condition were required on a fixed schedule. It would be checked for cracks within the nano-structures for safety reasons. The tools Julia would inspect were stationary and could not be moved. The Wizard knew that some of these tools were actually modifications to special components that would, with other components, convert the Firestone into a weapon. They were simply masquerading as maintenance tools and were built by the rebel espionage unit. Julia would be told that they are routine tools and monitoring devices. She would record their serial numbers then leave. The Wizard would ask Heather to look closely at the numbers so he could record them. When the facility was entered by one of his amphibious creatures at the bottom of the ocean he would have it confirm the serial number then sever the tool from its permanent position, and return it to the surface where it could be installed. This of course will require an intelligent creature which was currently the challenge.

While the Wizard was waiting for Julia to arrive at the facility, Sam was going about his other duties in an underground facility normally used for mining rubies, the Empire's primary source of income from the outside world. But the Wizard decided to sacrifice some of the islands income as they were already quite wealthy, having Royalty throughout

Europe as trading partners. The facility had been quickly converted to accommodate the Wizard's latest creature. Incubators had been moved in and when the creature was fully grown, which only took ten hours, it was moved to a secure holding pen another floor above closest to the surface.

Sam stopped recording the readings from the monitors for a moment and looked at the creature. This creature was injected with some of the Zapatsaurs bodily fluids, including blood. The hope was that when introduced during the early stages of its development, the creature would have greater intelligence when it was fully grown. It was also fire breathing thanks to the Wizard's genetic engineering. It wasn't much bigger than a full grown Zapatsaur and if it wasn't for its red scales and goats horns it might be close in appearance.

Sam began writing down the monitors measure of the creature's blood pressure on a piece of papyrus attached to a clipboard. The creature had a multifunction recording device wrapped around its neck attached to a cord which fed into the monitoring machine. It was looking good and healthy.

Sam of course was the Wizard's jack of all trades. He had come from a family of scientists who were also great athletes though the athletic attributes of the family failed to rub off on him. He was dressed casually, a white lab coat, brown pants and a white shirt which helped hold in a pot belly. He could sail a ship, carry out the Wizard's scientific duties, overlook the mining of rubies, and even supervise the agricultural needs of the island. The Empire's pear orchards nestled in the far south of the island was part of the Empire's goods for trade abroad. Sam organized those shipments on to the Empire's ship which he would have sea ready in another hour. His crew worked diligently in the cove to meet the deadline.

The news on the creature's development and current condition was excellent. Sam rubbed perspiration off his bald crown and entered the final recording on to his clipboard. He cursed as some of the ink from the quill splattered on to his lab coat which barely fit over his protruding belly. Sam was obsessed with cleanliness, and his lab coat was always as clean as brand new. He hung it up on a hook installed into the cave wall and put his clipboard beside it after removing the recorded results on papyrus. He would deliver the results to the Wizard.

Before climbing the thirty stone steps to the surface he looked back at the creature. It moved closer to the bars as though sensing Sam's curiosity. The creature opened its mouth to show Sam two rows of razor-sharp teeth. It made a low hissing sound then lowered its head and dragged its horns across the bars of the cage. Sam wasn't sure what it was trying to communicate, so he assumed it was hungry. He walked back over to the cage and reached into a basket close by pulling out a rabbit which had been cooked to perfection and tossed it into the cage. The creature lowered its powerful neck and pierced the meat with its right claw and held the rabbit up to its mouth consuming it in three bites. It moved back into the center of the cage, its long tail sweeping the ground as it turned and crouched down in a resting position. Sam turned and walked up the thirty steps where a fifteen by fifteen-foot wooden door securely locked would be opened to allow his departure.

Earlier that same morning Sally, Mitch and General Zen had set out from Azorka's port in the south. Sally's ship was always docked at this port which was surrounded by rock and landscape with a narrow passage way out. It was slightly larger compared to the other Azorkan ships. Sally's ship was grey in color and had twenty-four cannons that ran around the ship, with six large sails to catch the wind. There was a picture outside below the Captain's quarters large rear window and above the rudder. A painted picture of a red-headed lady standing in the ocean wielding an axe in one hand and holding arrows in the other. She was opposing a creature on the shore while behind her a Viking ship was sailing towards her.

General Zen had made a couple of slight modifications to Sally's ship. Both of the crow's nests as the pirates called them, were now closed at the top and had to be entered through a bottom door. Rungs had been placed in the mast to allow an effortless and safe entry. Once inside Zen's military officer would be able to fire a laser rifle through a slot which allowed the gun, secured on a swivel stand, to fire within a one-hundred eighty-degree angle. Two metal posts held up the roof of the enclosed crow's nest and a fire retardant had been brushed on the outside in anticipation of the Wizard's fire breathing creatures. General Zen had also taken the time to install Azorka's latest development which was a force field. The force field covered most of Sally's ship. The only vulnerable area of the ship was at the top which is also why the modified crow's nest was important. Ideally the creature or creatures would be destroyed before they reached this point given the range of the laser rifles.

Presently, Mitch, Sally and General Zen were on the top deck of Sally's ship and had already managed to sail twenty miles south. They were sitting on the benches built into the starboard side of the command deck. Everything sparkled like it was freshly painted and the wooden deck shone with a weekly treatment of linseed oil. A well-rested General Zen was explaining the ship's modifications.

"We should be prepared for all the military possibilities. Having the force field working for us is so important. I know the Empire has a hazel colored ship they use for shipping. It will more than likely have encountered pirates over the years. So, I assume that it has laser cannons as we do. The force field has been tested and can resist the most powerful laser blast. The two crow's nests will cover the vulnerable area above. Unfortunately, we haven't been able to wrap the force field around the entire ship yet." General Zen explained.

"That probably won't be necessary General. The Wizard's creatures are not intelligent and they'll wander into the field of fire without realizing the danger." Mitch said.

Sally was listening closely to the conversation. Her top priority was rescuing Heather. She knew for that to be a success, that they had to capture the Dragon Queen first. But where was Heather being held prisoner?

"Let's assume our plan works and the Wizard with his horde of creatures can't find the ship which will be far enough away and out of sight. We arrive outside the Dragon Queen's lair undetected. General Zen takes up a position to the side, outside of the Dragon Queen's cave entrance, and Mitch covers the other side. I hover in front of the cave entrance yelling at the Dragon Queen, threatening to take revenge for the kidnap of my sister. The Dragon Queen will think I've lost my mind. She'll figure me for an easy catch. She comes out as I trade my sword for my bow and fire off a tranquillizing arrow and both Mitch and Zen fire tranquillizing arrows from their positions outside her cave. She staggers as she passes out and we catch and entangle her in the fishing net Mitch has brought along. We take her back to the ship and chain her down in the hold. Now we must return to the island and find Heather and rescue her. The only problem is locating her." Sally finished.

With the exception of Sally, they stood up from their seats and started pacing back and forth on the deck as though this might help them recall massive amounts of intel on the Empire. A clue as to where the Wizard would hide Heather. The wind had picked up in a mostly grey sky and they were moving through the water a little quicker. The sound of the ocean against the ship and the seagulls singing above was all that could be heard.

CHAPTER 6

Julia had finally arrived at the secret location for southern Azorka's Firestone. The complex was made of concrete. From a distance, it's outer wall was horse-shoe shaped and the tower, with its circular staircase, looked like a fifty-foot high arrow sitting on top of half a pyramid. Julia had entered and began inspecting and cataloging the tools used for the Firestone. Her tour guide, a grey-haired fellow dressed in black pants and tunic, was patient as Julia stopped to write down the serial numbers. Heather watched closely and the Wizard saw the numbers on his screen which he meticulously recorded in his catalog. The entire process took about two hours and then Julia returned to the Aryan flying craft and departed for northern Azorka.

"Now Heather I need you to fast forward to five years into Julia's future. I need you to count forward. You will count from fifty to fifty-five and you will see Julia in that future when you reach fifty-five." The Wizard prompted.

Heather began counting and when she arrived at fifty-five, she screamed. This reaction took the Wizard by surprise. He looked back at his screen and immediately understood why. There on the screen were two of the Wizard's creatures from ten-thousand years ago flying over the same complex in a sky darkened with black and blue smoke. The Wizard remembered that day. The creatures had somehow escaped their pens and had to be put down. The creature closest to the complex's horse-shoe shaped outer wall and entrance had just bathed one of the female sentries in a jet stream of fire. The last tendrils of smoke leaked through razor sharp teeth inside of the large jaws of the attacking creature. All that remained of the sentry was a skull completely stripped of flesh with some of its hair still burning. The front entrance had been covered with what looked like a fishing net to prevent entry and it was also burning. In the background another of the Wizard's creatures flying high above, looked for more victims. The Wizard could see that the complex was still intact. The net was simply placed where it was to communicate the temporary closure of the complex. This meant that the completed Firestone for the south, was installed now in a pyramid. It had been moved and was fully functioning as a distributor of energy sent through the Earth's magnetic ley lines for the south. If it required maintenance, then the pyramid could receive energy sent through the ley lines by the north while the Firestone receives maintenance. Precise construction of both pyramids so that they could use the magnetic ley lines was the key to this successful form of energy distribution.

The Wizard now realized he should ask Heather to move forward in time to the day of the Firestone's return to the complex for maintenance. Unfortunately, Heather was sweating profusely from the shock. Julia had been approaching the complex on foot when she suffered the same shock now distorting the features on Heather's face. The Wizard decided to post-pone the experiment for one day to give Heather a little recovery time. She will be exhausted when he brings her out of this trance."Heather I'm going to count to ten. When you hear me say 'three' you will forget everything you saw Julia do. You will forget your ancestor Julia when you hear me say 'six'. When the Wizard reached 'ten' Heather lost that faraway expression in her eyes and she began stretching.

"What happened Wizard? I feel like I've been here for only ten minutes." Heather said. She removed the helmet and leaned forward to place it on the desk.

"Don't you remember Heather?" The Wizard asked.

"No, I don't remember…I was watching the crystal in your hand like you said then I began counting backwards and all of that feels like it took place ten minutes ago." Heather answered.

"You located the Aryan factory! We'll work together now and both Kingdoms will benefit!" The Wizard shouted, his facial expression jubilant.

Heather could tell by the Wizard's broad smile and enthusiasm that the experiment was a huge success. She felt a little groggy and sleepy at the present moment so couldn't share in the excitement.

"I'd like to rest now Wizard. Are we finished with the experiment?" She asked.

"We can finish up tomorrow. You could lay down for a while. Dinner will be ready in another three hours and I'll come knocking at your door to get you up in time for a real tasty meal."

Heather smiled and stood up. The Wizard walked past Heather and held the office door open for her. They walked down the stairs, through the reception room, to a front hallway which led outside where the sun had briefly poked out of the clouds. Heather looked up noting the position of the sun.

"How long was I in the trance helping to locate the Aryan factory?" She asked.

"About one hour." The Wizard lied.

The real length of time was closer to three hours. The Wizard didn't want Heather worrying that she was giving away too much information about Azorka. He felt one hour would be a reasonable time to locate the factory.

They arrived at the rear tower's front door and Heather gathered strength to walk up all the stairs to her room.

"I'll come back for you when it's dinner time." The Wizard said.

Heather smiled and said thanks then opened the door and began climbing the stairs to her room. The Wizard turned and walked back around to the castle's front door. He looked up at the sky still overcast but not windy, stretched his arms and was about to open the front door when he heard a shout. He turned and it was Sam running as fast as he could up the path to the front of the castle.

"Wizard we've got problems off our shore. I think a government vessel has stopped to take a look at our ships in the cove." Sam said between gasps of breath.

The Wizard was afraid of this happening but then this was also a perfect opportunity to test his creature. Leif and Sam must be permitted to leave on his mission without any challenges and in secrecy. Recovering the crystal skull from Haiti was too important.

"How big is this ship Sam." The Wizard asked.

"It's a smaller government ship, maybe a scout with about twenty-two cannons. The ship is about the same size as ours and the one we built for Leif. I was on my way to give you the good news about your new creature. I had just closed the big door when I noticed the ship. I stepped down on to the beach and saw that the ship's Captain had his telescope to his eye. He seemed to be looking at our ships trying to identify them, or so it appeared. He'll probably wait for us to set sail before he decides to confront us." Sam finished.

"I agree with you Sam. In fact, that Captain will probably play the hero demanding details of your sailing plan. When you don't comply, he'll try to sink two renegade ships which could help him get a promotion. If this kind of thinking guides his decisions it would be advantageous for us. It means he'll wait preferring to sink both our vessels rather than investigate by sending a party to shore. We'll delay our sailing time until tomorrow morning and we'll test the new creature tonight." The Wizard said.

Sam smiled about the new plan. He knew the Wizard would release the creature at sundown and they could access how efficient its oral stream of fire was at the expense of those nosey government agents. Sam chuckled to himself.

"I'll need to move forward with our testing. The picture boards we drew to educate the creature. The command process will come after this. The creature will avoid drifting into the line of cannon fire and will systematically destroy the ship by setting fire to the sails and decks. By the end of the night the ship and all its crew will have disappeared into a cloud of smoke." Sam said.

"I'll leave you to your task." The Wizard said.

Sam handed the papyrus with the creature's test results to the Wizard.

"Oh yes. Sam I'll join you in three hours. I think skipping dinner just to see how the attack goes will be worthwhile. I appreciate the good work you do for me Sam. When you recover the crystal skull your reward will be great and a holiday of your choice will also be available to you." The Wizard said.

He turned and opened the door as Sam rushed back down the path. He looked at the test results in the glow of the marble hallway. He was so happy with progress.

Upstairs in the tower an exhausted Princess paced back and forth. She had walked over to her window and saw a pudgy looking pirate, his bald head dripping with perspiration, speaking to the Wizard. He had a white shirt on with perspiration stains running down beneath the arms of the shirt and brown pants tucked into heavy leather boots that reached halfway up his fat calves. Both Kingdoms had agreed that they would not associate, for any purpose, with the outside world's criminal elements. The Wizard is violating agreements made for the best interests of both Kingdoms. Discovery was all the more likely through association with criminals who only respect personal gain.

Heather wondered if the Wizard could be trusted. She felt uneasy especially not being able to remember anything during the time she spent with the Wizard. Was she unknowingly giving away important information that might compromise the security of Azorka.

Heather looked at her control console again wrapped around her white robe. The switch that Ted had installed reflected light from her room's lamp and seemed to be begging her to activate it. Should she risk the life of her Zapatsaur. She thought if it could just get to her window undetected then they could slip away together unnoticed. It would be easy to kick out the decorative wooden bars on her window and hop on to her Zapatsaur. The night guard was by the tower's front door and wouldn't be able to hear the wooden pieces falling to the ground. Heather sat back down on her bed. She clicked the switch. She had to and with that final thought she fell back on the bed and was fast asleep after another minute.

In Azorka the Zapatsaur population had absorbed the details of the tragedy. Two Zapatsaurs were brutally murdered by the Wizard's fire breathing creature. Zapatsaurs were grieving individually at home in their caves. Heather's Zapatsaur sat crouched up on a large bed of pillows. It looked around the eight-hundred square foot area of this home built long ago by the Azorkans. They had built tunnels and caves for the Zapatsaurs, although the Zapatsaurs had the technology to build their own secret tunnel to the inner city something they hid from the Azorkans. This home had been laser cut into the mountain and featured a dome shaped ceiling. The entrance was fourteen-feet high and a short hallway led into the dome shaped living area which had a twenty-five-foot high ceiling. This Zapatsaur's choice of furniture was mostly cushions and pillows which were strung together to form a chair or couch, the latter doubling as a bed. One table was sufficient for dining from a storage cooler.

Heather's Zapatsaur got up and walked to the entrance. It wanted to stretch a little and see what the weather was doing. Outside the sun was in the west and only partially visible because of heavy cloud cover. The wind had died down. The Zapatsaur turned and walked back through the hallway and unfolded the curtain that covered the hallway entrance, and kept the weather out. It was about to take a drink from the cooler when all of a sudden it felt a pulse coming from the belt Heather had put around its neck. The Zapatsaur stood frozen to the spot. It felt another pulse, and after another minute the signal interval was a continuous pulse every twenty seconds. The Zapatsaur realized the new locating device had been activated by Heather and that she needed help. Heather's Zapatsaur knew what should be done immediately.

The Zapatsaur called out a telepathic message requesting a meeting with two top ranking elders. The telepathic message to the elders included a three-dimensional picture of the device installed on Heather's control console and the belt wrapped around its neck. The elders were also concerned for Heather because of the length of time she'd been held captive and saw that this was a locating device now being used for an emergency. The Zapatsaur telepathy had evolved after millions of years and descriptive three-dimensional pictures were sent so perfectly detailed that in some cases it felt like you were in the mental illustration. The imagery that was taken from Mitch's recollection of the two Zapatsaurs killed was so accurate that it intensified the grief of the Zapatsaur population. Every Zapatsaur felt their final emotions before they perished.

Heather's Zapatsaur left its cave and flew down the mountain until it reached the fifteen-foot tall entrance to the elder's cave. It entered and folded its wings flat against its back then assumed an upright position and began walking down a thirty-degree slope. The floor and walls were lasered and smooth. Heather's Zapatsaur arrived at a lower level where two elders were already waiting in a conference room, a short distance away. There were no doors to open or close. No activity in the hallway no noise and no need for privacy as nothing would be hidden from the population. Secrecy in the Zapatsaur's society was never necessary. Unlike many societies on Earth, the Zapatsaurs were selfless and always thinking of the good for the community. After a couple more, turns in the tunnel Heather's Zapatsaur had reached the conference room. It was a half-moon shaped room with two elders waiting patiently, seated at a bench their scaly forearms resting on a large wooden table. Heather's Zapatsaur gave a nod of its head in greeting and approached the table. It preferred to stand in order to make its case for a rescue mission. It thanked the elders for assembling on such short notice and for interrupting their grieving for the loss of the two Zapatsaurs.

Heather's Zapatsaur began sending telepathic imagery which displayed a variety of scenarios for extreme danger within the mission. The danger of running into the fire breathing creatures the Wizard had created and the possibility of encountering the Dragon Queen. Most important of all, Heather was at risk and at the mercy of the Wizard. There was even a possibility that the Wizard would be bold enough to force an operation changing Heather into a creature as loathsome as the Dragon Queen.

After a short while of considering all that has been presented the two elders were decided. Heather was well loved in their society and this transmission from the locating device was a desperate request for help. The two elders sent Heather's Zapatsaur a picture of Sally's ship with Mitch and Zen aboard standing on the upper deck. Sally's ship had sailed half the distance to the Empire's Kingdom on a choppy ocean. The telepathic imagery showed Heather's Zapatsaur descending from the clouds and arriving on the main deck of Sally's ship to join them. It pointed to the belt around its neck and Sally walked up to see and confirmed that this was Ted's device that Heather had briefly talked about. Communication should not be a problem on this mission and the Zapatsaurs purpose would be understood.

Heather's Zapatsaur welcomed the suggestion it should join the rescue mission already underway. The Zapatsaur elders were aware of the rescue effort, the locating device, and that Sally had been told of it by Heather. This knowledge would be helpful for the Zapatsaur's success. Heather's Zapatsaur would have proposed a different kind of mission but it also knew that the elders believed that this was the best kind of help for the rescue team.

The elders believed that Mitch and General Zen were the most informed about their enemy's motives and methods. Heather's Zapatsaur thanked the two elders and left the room beginning its walk up to the cave entrance. Cool air filled its nostrils at the entrance and it took a moment to stretch. Unfolding its wings, Heather's Zapatsaur looked in the southerly direction it must fly then took off into the cloudy late afternoon sky. Estimated arrival time for Sally's ship was sundown.

Sam had reached the entrance to the underground facility for the new creature. The foreign ship was still off shore, its sails were down and the anchor dropped. He opened the large door just wide enough to squeeze through so that the movement would not attract the attention of the crew aboard the ship. Once inside Sam hurried down the steps to the creature's cage. He walked up to the cage and reached into the food bucket pulling out a cooked pheasant. Sam passed it through the bars. The creature impaled the pheasant breast with its right claw and raised it to a salivating mouth full of sharp teeth. In one delicious bite the pheasant was gone and Sam could have sworn he saw a smile of satisfaction stretching those reptilian lips. Sam reached down to a table with a stack of twenty by thirty-inch boards. He pulled up the first educational board. This was a picture of a ship much like the one outside. Sam held the board still so that the creature could memorize the image. Then Sam changed the educational board and on the new board was a picture of himself and the Wizard feeding the creature a pheasant. The artwork was excellent and Sam thought himself lucky to have a crew member amongst them they could rely on for artistic precision. It was critical that the creature recognized and understood each educational board.

The picture of a smiling Sam and Wizard providing food for the creature suggested friends, family, security and that the creature should respect, protect and obey. That was the subliminal Sam had hoped would be understood and remain in the creature's memory. The next picture showed a mean looking Captain dressed in the uniform of his nation, in this case Portugal. The Captain had a threatening expression, frowning and scowling, standing next to his ship on the dock. A large flag with the Portuguese emblem on it was also in the picture. The next educational board showed the creature attacking the Captain and his ship. Fire streamed out of the creature's mouth surrounding the enemy Captain and catching fire to the ship's sails and deck. The next educational board was a repeat of the creature being fed by a smiling Wizard and Sam who were now holding cooked pheasants up to the cage for the creature to eat. The intention was for this to become the job well done and reward board in the mind of the creature.

If this board followed a board depicting the creature in an action or command then the creature's action was positive and upon completion worthy of a reward. So, a very basic psychology lesson for the youthful fire breathing creature.

While the creature's lessons were in progress, the Wizard had left instructions with the lady servant to wake Heather in another hour and escort her to the reception room's dining area for dinner. The lady servant would join Heather for dinner and conversation. The lady servant may ask questions about life in Azorka and answer simple questions about life in the Empire's Kingdom. She would not divulge details of missions with the Wizard, like the recent capture of the baby Zapatsaur. Perhaps an unnecessary precaution as Heather wasn't aware of Amy's involvement yet. The lady servant would appear to lack knowledge about the Empire's conquests and objectives.

The Wizard arrived at the large entrance to the facility used for the creature. The sun was going down and the shadows from overhead trees were creeping towards the door. The Wizard could see the ship about four hundred yards away. He opened the large door just a crack and slipped down those rocky steps to join Sam and the educational lessons now in session.

Meanwhile aboard the ship for rescue and capture, events were about to take a turn for the better. Sally was the first to see their visitor.

"Hey Mitch. Looks like we have company." Sally hollered.

She pointed skyward at Heather's Zapatsaur. It dropped out of the sky descending to the main deck. The Zapatsaur landed with a gentle thump and looked up at the amazed General Zen Sally, and Mitch who all looked down from the upper command deck. Heather's Zapatsaur folded its wings and stood upright pointing to the belt wrapped around its neck just as the elders had suggested to do.

"General Zen, if I'm correct that's the new and untested locator device Heather briefly told me about. Ted's division developed it and Heather placed the belt around her Zapatsaur's neck for safe keeping before they could test it. She told me the story when I asked how her date went that evening." Sally said.

"That's what it looks like from here and if the Zapatsaur has flown here to show us than Heather has activated it on her end." The General said.

"I agree with that quick deduction. Let's go find out." Mitch said.

They poured down the upper decks stairs and walked up to the Zapatsaur. The General reached up and felt the belt. There was a pulse every twenty seconds. The signal interval was consistent, a design feature working perfectly he thought. Mitch was close behind him and Sally moved forward to pet the creature's neck.

The General was still examining the belt around the neck of Heather's Zapatsaur.

"The belt is giving off three pulses per minute like it should be doing when in use." The General said.

"I'm going to get you something to eat while you rest." Sally said as she stroked the neck of Heather's Zapatsaur. She turned and walked away disappearing into a room below the upper deck, which they were using as a kitchen.

"Zen could I assume that if the locater is functioning the way it is supposed to than this not a false alarm?" Mitch asked.

"I agree Mitch. Heather must need our help and made the decision to activate the switch on her control console." The General replied.

Sally came back out with a fully cooked grouse she had passed up for dinner. She brought it to the Zapatsaur sitting in a resting position on the deck. The Zapatsaur reached forward with its right hand piercing the grouse with its claws. Sally watched as their hungry friend devoured the wild meat in a couple of bites.

"General, what will happen as Heather's Zapatsaur gets closer to Heather's location. Will the belt pulse more or less."? Sally asked.

"The pulse rate will increase as the distance between Heather's control console and her Zapatsaur decreases. When Heather is only twenty yards away it will be pulsating ten times per minute around our friend's neck." The General answered.

"I think wondering how to rescue Heather just got a little easier." Sally said.

"I think so to. We'll find out tomorrow night after we've formulated a plan. We will also be setting out to capture the Dragon Queen and maybe both plans can be worked together." Mitch suggested.

"I'll rework our plan a little so it will include the participation of Heather's Zapatsaur. I want to make sure every possible precaution can be taken so that the Zapatsaur can carry out the mission with the least amount of danger." The General said.

"That's good thinking and of course we'll need Heather's Zapatsaur with us in the morning for the briefing after you and Mitch have formulated a new plan." Sally said.

Sally's mood was suddenly elevated with confidence the turn of events had instilled.

"Let's get some rest. Tomorrow is shaping up to be a big day. We'll draw up the plan in the morning." Mitch said.

With that suggestion they retired early just as a red sun was being doused by a hungry ocean.

The Wizard knew that the creature's comprehension of commands was a very important part of the educational process. He learned that the hard way ten-thousand years ago when Julia had stumbled on two of his creatures that had gone out of control and had to be put down by laser rifle. Fortunately for Julia she escaped unharmed.

The Wizard had developed an orientation session using the crystal he had swung back and forth in order to induce a trance then reviewed the lessons with the creature. That's what he was doing now beside a beaming Sam who had successfully completed the educational sessions. The Wizard's process was making sure that the lessons would stick in the creature's mind.

Sam was surprised with his results. The creature had pointed to the correct educational board during Sam's sessions ten out of ten times. The creatures intelligent use of its hand for eating and during testing when it closed together the three fingers to form a pointer, suggested that it may have even greater potential for the future. Sam couldn't wait to further its education after the mission. He was beginning to bond with the creature and even contemplated being its rider in the future.

The creature's attention was fixed on the crystal the Wizard was swinging back and forth and the lessons he repeated in his deep voice. The creature stood there frozen to the spot so it would seem. The creatures large ten-foot tail was still and no longer sweeping the floor of its cage. When upright the creature stood twenty-feet tall. Armor tough segmented body, muscular legs and arms with lethal size claws suggested a powerful fighting machine when unleashed. It's short goat like horns caught the reflection of the Wizard's crystal as he became completely silent. He was attempting telepathic communication with the creature and had just begun to smile with what must have been the results of that silent test.

Despite the overcast and sometimes windy day the sun had gone down a bright red which Heather thought unusual as she stretched in front of the window. Large shadows cast by the Wizard's castle cloaked the walk ways but Heather could just make out a lady walking towards the tower. A couple minutes later there was a knock at her door. Heather opened her door and the Wizard's lady servant did a quick curtsey and introduced herself as 'Amy'.

"The Wizard has been called away on another errand and has asked me to dine with you tonight. I've come to take you to dinner." Amy said.

Amy wore a seventeenth century orange and yellow dress over a pair of yellow pants with blue square toed shoes and silver buckles. Heather thought her color coordination was comical. She was an attractive lady who didn't look any older than thirty and although she had premature grey hair, there was a youthful twinkle in her light brown eyes when she smiled.

"That's fantastic. I just woke up and I'm hungry enough to eat a horse!" Heather replied.

Amy was amused by Heather's remark and almost began to laugh out loud. She would enjoy the company of this strange young lady dressed in her long white robe over white tunic and pants. Amy thought the absence of color in her wardrobe was unusual.

"We'll be having pheasant breasts stuffed with spinach and the Wizard has made sure we enjoy some English beef. He knows how fascinated you are with those people. It's a prime rib roast and I've been cooking it for the last two hours." Amy said.

Heather thought a prime rib roast was the most delicious serving of beef and her mouth began to water.

"I'm looking forward to this treat. Amy lead the way."

Heather shut her door and followed Amy down the steps. Outside a few dark clouds had rolled in overhead but it wasn't windy. They walked around the front of the castle and through the same orange marble hallway until arriving in the reception room. Heather could smell the most delicious aroma coming from the dining table. A couple of candles arranged in the middle of the table helped the silver dishes to sparkle. She took her seat and Amy sat across from her. The prime rib roast was already sliced up and stacked on a silver serving tray which had a candle under the dish to keep the beef warm. The pheasant breasts were arranged much the same way except that a silver top plate covered them and the candle was much smaller beneath the dish. Oven potatoes and carrots were also cooked to perfection.

Heather thought Amy was a very talented cook. The dinner was fantastic, each tender slice of the medium rare roast incredibly delicious. For the next ten minutes both ladies ate in silence, enjoying second helpings of the savory dish they found the most delicious. Amy looked over to see if Heather was enjoying the meal.

"What do you think. How do you like the beef."? Amy asked.

"This is fantastic. I can't wait to try the pheasant." Heather answered.

"There's some cheese sauce here if you need it and this bowl in front of me has gravy for the roast if you would like to try it. I know the English put gravy on their potatoes. Personally, I think it adds flavor to the potato but covers up the great taste of the meat." Amy offered.

"Thank you, Amy."

Heather went back to finishing her prime rib slice while Amy reached for the pheasant. She extended her reach by standing and grabbing the gravy bowl so she wouldn't have to bother Amy for it, then drowned her potatoes and carrots in what she thought was the most incredibly tasty gravy. After another fifteen minutes the two ladies had finished the meal with no room for dessert. Heather looked around the reception room with its various art works and frescos that adorned the walls.

"Do all the citizens in the Empire live underground." Heather asked.

Amy was waiting for Heather's curiosity to change the topic for conversation. In preparation for this eventuality she had rehearsed a brief overview of the Empire's society to satisfy it.

"Our society lives just below the surface hidden from the outside world. This helps maintain secrecy and that barren look to our island. If we were living above ground there could be reason to invade. As it is, governments and pirates steer clear. There doesn't appear to be anything to profit from by dropping anchor to investigate. The island looks deserted with the exception of the Wizard's castle which is well concealed by the natural terrain."

"The outside world is not aware that we do a lot of mining for jewels underground and the abundance of rubies on our island is what keeps our bank rich so that we can purchase goods from the outside world. Further south we have a small but productive orchard of pear trees tucked between two large rocky and shrub covered hills. The rest of our food is grown underground in what we call green houses. Everyone is well cared for and in turn work well for the Empire. The Wizard is a better character than you think. After the war, all the rebel leaders had perished and the Wizard was the only survivor capable of leading the Kingdom. As a monarch, he does well for the people. The homes out there in the field southwest from here house our policy makers and military commanders."

"They are domed and open to the sky like your homes but unlike your homes they are submerged twenty-feet below the surface so that the dome is not visible on the surface unless your flying over. There are two levels designed for a family of four. Our people still walk above ground if they wish, although most of the population have become sensitive to the intensity of the sun. A great many work underground either mining or attending to food production in our greenhouses on the upper levels. Our schools operating for our children are domed and submerged beneath the surface like our homes. There's a network of clean underground concrete pathways leading from home to school or home to market place for our people. There is even a very modern metropolis further below that some of our people enjoy living in, complete with gyms for exercise, swimming pools, and many other people orientated venues." Amy continued.

"Our children learn from an early age of the Kingdoms secrecy and that the outside world will someday come close to destroying the planet with its lust for war. In the summer, the children learn to lay flat on the ground if they notice a ship sailing by when they are above ground playing sports. Though this is infrequent and we have sports arenas below ground for them. They realize secrecy now is essential if the Kingdom is to save the world from war. To obtain this goal we must rule the planet and our children must grow up with great knowledge and leadership skills." Amy finished.

Heather was mesmerized by Amy's speech.

"That doesn't sound so bad except the part about ruling the planet. We've always maintained that the outside world should grow and mature into the technology we could provide. Our agents keep a close eye on the progress and leadership of the outside world and report regularly on those events. It is our hope that in the future we can work with a leader from the outside world whose priority is peace on earth." Heather said.

"What do you do for fun when you're not working for the Wizard?"

Heather thought it best to change the subject now that she knew Amy would probably disagree with her Kingdom's approach to the outside world.

"I have an interest in what I call 'sword-play' and I'm practicing to be a great swords-lady." Amy replied. Heather looked around the room remembering that she had seen a coat of arms on the wall. It was ten feet directly behind Amy. The decorated shield, two Griffins holding up a castle colored red and black, was crossed by two finely crafted swords. The swords were about three and a half feet long and finely engraved.

"I would like to teach you what I know if you can spare thirty minutes after I help you clear the table." Heather offered.

Amy's expression brightened up with enthusiasm and her brown eyes flew wide at the mention of swords ladyship lessons.

"Great. I'd like to learn more moves."

They both got up and cleared the dishes from the table to the wash area in the kitchen. Amy decided that washing the dishes could wait.

Amy walked over to the coat of arms and stood on a chair close by to release the two swords from the hooks that held them in place across the decorated shield. She got down from her chair and over to Heather waiting by the table. She held out the two identical swords for Heather to choose. Heather took the sword in her left hand then began swinging it back and forth to get familiar with its weight and length. Heather knew she was at least five inches taller than Amy and that Amy's reach would not be the same as hers. She factored this into her lesson.

"First thing to do is to position yourself across from your opponent. You should match their steps and be aware of them choosing to strike at any moment." Heather said.

"Now take a strike at me. Do a forward thrust when you think the time is right and I'll show you how I deflect it."

Amy positioned herself and matched Heather step for step, their swords clashing together as they moved about the reception room. Amy waited until she thought she could catch Heather off guard. Suddenly, Amy thrust forward with her sword for a killing shot at Heather's stomach. Heather quickly dodged to the side and hit Amy's sword at the same time. Then she brought her sword up to Amy's neck and held it there, noticing the look of surprise on Amy's face.

"That was good Amy. I wasn't expecting that much alacrity. Such a briskness has already instilled itself from your earlier lessons. You could become a very challenging opponent in the future."[A very dangerous opponent she thought]

"So, a simple side step removing yourself from the kill spot and at the same time I used my sword to hit yours and change its direction, then holding my sword to your kill spot before you could recover your direction." Heather stated.

Amy smiled enjoying this fun and impressed with Heather's tutoring.

"What if your opponent fakes a forward thrust and instead brings their sword down on top of your head." Amy asked.

"Than you hold your sword in a parallel position above your head." A deeper voice called to them from the hall.

Both ladies turned their heads in surprise and there in the entrance way from the dimly lit hall stood a smiling Leif.

Amy had already met Leif and gave him a quick curtsy and smile. Heather faced him and gave a traditional style fencing bow. She was surprised to see this unexpected visitor and remembered that the Wizard had instructed her to introduce herself as his niece.

"My name's Heather sir. I'm the Wizard's niece on a short visit with my uncle." She lied.

Leif returned the bow and said,"I'm glad to meet you. My name's Leif and I work for the Wizard abroad. I'm expecting to set sail tomorrow.

I didn't mean to surprise or intrude dear ladies. I was just on my way to the kitchen to get a snack before I go to bed. Need lots of sleep and energy for an early start."

"There's some prime rib roast still warm and waiting for you in the Kitchen. You just have to slice it up." Amy offered.

At this mention Leif quickly walked past Heather and Amy on his way to the kitchen.

"Heather, I would like to continue this lesson with you another time." Amy said.

"We could try tomorrow afternoon if that would work for you. I'm sure I'll be done assisting the Wizard with his experiment by then." Heather suggested.

"That should be fine. I'll mention it to the Wizard. Leif turning up unexpected wasn't something I was prepared for. But his arrival did remind me that I should go over my list and make sure I haven't short changed him on supplies for his trip." Amy said.

"I'll stay and help you do the dishes." Heather offered.

"Oh no please. I know the Wizard wants you to be his guest." Amy said.

"I won't let you lift a finger. However, I have a short story I'd like you to read. One of the Empire's top students had won an award for his composition and I want your opinion." Amy said.

Heather gave a quick nod of her head, a silent yes to the request. She had hoped to engage Amy in more conversation by helping her wash dishes and her other duties. She walked over to the shield on the wall and placed her sword on the floor below it. She walked back and took the twenty-five-page short story Amy handed her.

"I want to thank you for a dinner and evening I truly enjoyed. I want you to think of me as your friend and tomorrow, if all goes well, we'll continue the lessons for more advanced swordplay." Heather said.

Amy thanked Heather than turned to go back to the kitchen. Heather decided to go back to her room. She went out through the front hallway into a dark and silent night.

CHAPTER 7

This was incredible he thought. The Wizard was certain that he had received a telepathic communication from the creature. The imagery was of the ship waiting outside down to every detail. The creature had seen this imagery, most likely, from both of their minds, it didn't come from the educational board. It had already achieved telepathy in such a short period of time. The Wizard now wondered if the creature could also communicate with Sam. Could the creature open a section of his brain and broadcast his message. He turned in the dim light to a silent but excited Sam.

"Sam, I want to see if you can receive a telepathic communication from the creature." He said.

Sam looked a little surprised when he heard this. He knew Zapatsaurs read human thoughts but they never sent them messages. The Wizard had only introduced a small part of the Zapatsaur DNA while creating this creature so he would assume its telepathy would be limited to the norm. The Zapatsaur would alter flight direction by simply reading the thoughts of the rider. They could arrive precisely on time when the rider needed help. They were believed to have a fifty-mile radius for their telepathy but after that the rider would disappear from their psychological radar. The Zapatsaurs didn't send a telepathic message for help when the Dragon Queen captured the baby Zapatsaur, after fifty miles into the chase. They would still be alive if they had requested a laser equipped squadron of riders to help them on the island.

"How do I begin Wizard." Sam asked.

"Send a message to the creature by thinking about the ship's Captain, then ask the creature to send you that image." The Wizard instructed.

Sam looked at the creature and it moved its large neck until those piercing green eyes were just inches away from Sam. He thought about the ship's Captain as he appeared in the distance with his Captains hat and the telescope in his hand. Sam painted the picture in his mind complete with the color of his uniform and as much facial features that could be seen from a distance through a telescope. Sam included the imagery of the Captain holding the telescope to his eye examining Leif's ship. Without uttering a word, Sam asked the creature to send him the image of the Captain. A few minutes passed. Sam was patiently waiting for the communication wondering when the imagery would appear in his mind. After about five minutes of waiting and a second request for the creature to send the image Sam had to concede.

"No worry Sam, but we had to try. I'm receiving communication from the creature and the implications for the future are enormous. I believe it can open up my mind, an automatic action perhaps it's not aware of, and that's how we can communicate. People can send suggestions, on the planet I'm from Sam, but we can't accomplish telepathy to this extent." The Wizard finished.

Sam was the only human being that he trusted with this knowledge. Sam's contribution and hard work for the Empire had gradually worked him closer to the Wizard's secrets to such an extent that Sam couldn't help but believe that any other explanation could explain the phenomena he witnessed.

"It's so young to have progressed this far. I'll be the creature's future rider. After it gets rid of the ship the creature will return with us to the castle. You'll need to get ahead of us and lock the door to the tower, when we depart. I don't want our guests to be aware of the creature. Hopefully, they will both be sleeping by the time we leave here. I'll put a large blanket over the creature which will allow me to explain it as a horse should either Leif or Heather be looking out their window. Amy will see the creature and probably fall in love with it. The creature will be well cared for, like my own son." The Wizard finished.

The Wizard moved forward and unlocked the door to the creature's cage. Sam and the Wizard walked backwards slowly keeping their eyes on the creature's movements. The creature walked out of the cage, towering twenty-feet above them in its upright position with its wings folded back. The creature's red color was barely visible in the dim light. The Wizard looked up at the creature meeting its luminous green eyes and began his mental communication of the task at hand which was destroying the ship outside. A minute went by and the Wizard gave a nod of his head as a signal for them to go. Sam turned and led the way up the stone steps to the large door above. His footfalls echoed on the steps of the corridor where a tall ceiling was able to fit the bulk of the creature.

Sam looked back at the creature following close behind him. Its legs must have been five feet long with twenty-four-inch feet ending in sharp claws large enough to pierce a human chest. The arms were rippled in muscle just like the legs but four feet in length. Powerful hands, three digits like the feet, had sharp lethal claws just about as long as the claws on its feet. Large green eyes looked down, almost quizzically, regarding Sam as though wondering why he was examining so closely. Sam quickly turned around, not wanting to spook the creature and looked ahead as they neared the exit door. He skipped up a couple of steps and walked over to the wheel that would open the door wide enough for the creature to fit through. Sam began turning the wheel. The door creaked and slowly began to open. It was dark so the ship wouldn't see the door open on an overcast night which covered the light of the moon. The Wizard and the creature stepped out into the night.

Sam reversed the wheels direction closing the door then squeezed out through a narrow gap he left himself, pushing the door closed once outside.

The Wizard and the creature stood motionless before him, standing in the shadows of the beach, looking in the direction of the ship. Suddenly the creature walked up to the water's edge and unfolded its twelve-foot wings. It ran a couple quick steps and took off. It seemed to spring into the air, and stayed low by flying about six-feet above the ocean surface, creeping towards the ship. At a distance of about one-hundred yards, it swiftly accelerated to an incredible speed and flew directly upwards until it disappeared into the darkness.

On the ship the sailors were attending to their duties while other crew members kept watch. The crewman on the main deck with the telescope had seen movement from the shore but because it was so dark outside he couldn't make out any details. He thought he could see something moving towards him on the water. The crewman was questioning his own eyes when suddenly he saw a dark shadow race upwards into the sky. The shape blotting out the natural background in this instant was the length of two lifeboats. He knew something was wrong so he called up to the Captain who was on the upper deck.

"Captain Domingo. Please come here sir. The crewman shouted in Portuguese."

The Captain was close to fifty with a dark black beard long enough to cover half his neck. He was in uniform and carried his six-foot athletic build with military pride and eloquence down the stairway from the command deck to the starboard side of the lower deck. The Captain was a little perturbed with the interruption. He had planned to rest for a couple of hours. However, he respected the diligence of those on watch.

"What is it crewman." He replied in Portuguese.

The Captain walked up to the crewman who was clean shaven and wearing a dark blue corporal's uniform.

"Sir please take the telescope and train it on this direction and tell me if you see anything. I thought I saw a large shape approaching the ship then it seemed to rise up swiftly into the sky and disappeared. It must be the overcast weather and infrequent moonlight that played a trick on my eyes." He said.

The Captain looked a little confused but took the telescope and as he raised it to his eye a shout rang out."Captain. Above your head sir. Something coming in fast." The alarmed crewman from the upper deck called out.

The Captain looked up at a huge shape descending swiftly from the sky and froze in fear at the sight. The creature had a huge head with horns and its green eyes were like luminous lanterns shining down on its target. It opened its hideously largemouth filled with razor sharp teeth releasing a deadly stream of fire as it approached the ship's top mast. The rolled-up sails above the Captain's head caught on fire. Crewmen were running and shouting about extinguishing the fire, while at the same time Portuguese soldiers were firing their muskets and rifles at the creature in an attempt to kill it. The creature moved far too quickly for this attempt to be effective. It flew upward into the night disappearing from the burning ship. There was a gathering of crewmen at the bow of the ship where a cannon had been rolled over in the hopes of catching the creature in its sights. Suddenly, the creature dropped out of the sky and landed feet first and upright in the middle of those crewmen. The twenty-foot tall creature folded its wings and standing upright began striking the crewmen with its powerful arms and three of them were sent over board falling into a freezing ocean, sixteen-feet below. The remaining two crewmen were to shocked to move and stared up at the creature. The creature opened those jaws and moved its neck down to meet their frightened expressions and hissed like a snake about to strike. With lightning speed, it reached down and grasping the cannon in its powerful hands it raised the cannon above its head like it was a toy and tossed it overboard. Both crewmen regained their mobility and turning in terror they ran down the main deck to where the Captain had positioned himself on the starboard side of the ship. The creature followed while at the same time sending a stream of fire to remaining masts, sails and the deck which was shaking with its every foot fall. The fleeing crewmen decided to take their chances with the frigid ocean and dived overboard to avoid the creature's stream of fire moving towards them.

The Captain looked up at the approaching horror and decided to abandon ship. He had taken the precaution of lowering a life boat with two of his crew members. It was positioned below with the two crewmen waiting for the Captain to join them. The Captain climbed over the starboard side rail and lowered himself to a narrow walk way which ran the length of the ship where the lower level of cannons was situated. The shutters were open and the barrels pointing out to sea, but no one was left on board to fire those silent guns.

The creature looked down at the Captain as he lowered himself to the walkway. The Captain braced himself for the assault. He'd fired his last shot and didn't have a weapon to fight back with. Fortunately, the creature passed by and continued setting the upper deck on fire as the Wizard had instructed. The Captain lowered himself into the lifeboat where the two shivering crewmen were waiting for him. He was glad this was a surveillance mission requiring a minimal number of crewmen and soldiers. The entire Portuguese army would have been wiped out by this creature if the opportunity presented itself.

"We will pick up the others." The Captain whispered in Portuguese.

The two crewmen's teeth were chattering as much from shock as the effects of the freezing ocean. The Captain decided to take the oars himself and quietly pick up the rest of the crew without the creature being aware of their escape. He didn't know the creature was no longer interested in the crew. The creature was hovering in front of the bow of the ship, about two feet from the surface of the ocean. It wound up its right arm and drove it through the thick wood of the ship. Withdrawing its arm, the creature could see the water rushing into the ship and was satisfied the ship would sink in a short matter of time. It flew up into the night sky towards an overjoyed Wizard and Sam waiting on the shore.

It landed in front of them knowing how happy and proud both men were about the successful completion of the creature's first mission.

"This calls for a celebration my friend." The Wizard shouted.

The creature had already seen the image of the prime rib roast in the Wizard's mind and its mouth began to water. Sam could just about swear it was smiling as the Wizard placed a large blanket he had brought up from below over the creature. The frightening features of the creature would be covered up and the Wizard would walk ahead of it as though leading a horse.

"I'll run ahead of you Wizard and lock the tower door. With any luck your guests will be sleeping. After I send the sentry away on an errand, I'll remain outside the tower door until you've got the creature into the castle, then unlock the door and join you back in your reception room." Sam said.

"Perfect Sam." The Wizard replied.

He watched Sam race up the dark path which led to the castle. When Sam had disappeared over a small rise on the path he began leading the creature back to the castle.

Sam was close to his destination and in another couple of minutes he turned a corner and the dark shadow of the tower crossed his path. The window was dark where Heather's room was but Leif's window was on the other side and Sam didn't know if he was still up. Probably not though, considering tomorrows mission. Sam walked over to the stone path and followed it to the towers entrance where a sentry stood guard. The sentry saw Sam approach and came to attention.

"Evening sir." He said. The sentry was dressed in dark clothing with a black leather vest and a black powder pistol attached to his belt. He was clean shaven and about thirty years of age, average height.

"Good evening Eric." Sam said.

"I need you to patrol the approach to the front yard for the next fifteen minutes. It's a couple hundred yards from here but a pathway we believe the intruders used the other night. Please give me a written report on your suggestions for incorporating it into the patrol routine in the morning. For now, I'll stand guard here for fifteen minutes. That will be all." Sam instructed.

The sentry went off to do as Sam had instructed.

Sam locked the door to the tower then moved over a couple of feet, away from the view Leif would have from his window, which fortunately was dark. Sam moved against the wall and remained in the shadows waiting for the Wizard and the creature to appear.

Leif had overeaten which usually caused him to sleep afterwards. Heather had read the short story from the Empire's student then gone to bed.

Strangely enough, Heather had a dream about the story in more vivid detail then she normally would in a dream. The story was about a young student from Azorka who had gone out to fish for his father who was sick in bed with a cold. The student's boat had been caught in a storm and he was ship wrecked on the Empire's island. A student from the Empire who was the same age as the boy from Azorka had found him and brought him back to his family in their underground home. The next day the Azorkan boy was invited to school where he learned of the Empire's desire to unite with Azorka in order to stop the outside world from destroying the planet.

Heather woke up during the middle of the night after her dream. Something in her memory was tickling her conscious thought. She knew that she had devoted enough time to thinking over the possibilities of a truce with the Empire. Right now, she would have to concentrate on her planned departure. She knew that her Zapatsaur was on its way but that two-hundred miles of ocean separate them. The Zapatsaur would fly towards the Empire's island and when it was fifty miles away from Heather it would pick up her thoughts. That was the moment to think over and over again,"Rescue me below my window one hour after sunset tomorrow." Heather thought this over and over until she fell asleep again.

Upstairs in the castle, Amy was removing her light brown contact lenses. Her hidden room, concealed by tapestry, was beside the Wizard's office. The contact lenses Amy wore were kept secret. They were not uncomfortable but necessary to keep up appearances around Azorkans and the people of the Empire. Amy's eyes were a dark navy blue and so dark they looked black. She had the same color eyes and grey skin as the Wizard. A pad of flesh colored powder concealed her skin color. It was important that people see her as human. Only Sam was aware that both she and the Wizard shared the same origins and he didn't ask questions when it came down to what's best for the Empire. That's why he was the Wizard's most trusted scientist and General.

Amy placed her contact lenses in their case and returned them to the top of her eight-drawer gold gilded dresser that Leif had 'acquired' from one of his trips to France. Her room was beautifully decorated with a queen size bed complete with gold gilded headboard and needlepoint chairs arranged around her six-hundred square foot apartment. Outside, her door was covered with a portion of red colored tapestry depicting another European hunting scene. On closer examination, the trained eye could see the rectangular border cut for the door.

Amy sat back down on a small but comfortable chair she had placed in front of the bed. She stretched out her legs, relaxing and glad to be done with the day's chores. Then she heard some commotion from downstairs. The Wizard must be returning from his mission except she was sure she heard heavier feet pounding the floor. She walked past a painting of herself and the Wizard in Rome two-thousand years ago. They had enjoyed their brief trip together so paid the artist with a priceless ruby to commemorate the experience on canvas. Amy opened the door and walked down the short hallway to the steps which led to the reception room below.

At the bottom of the steps she opened the door and was astonished by the scene in the reception room. The Wizard was removing a blanket from what looked like one of his creatures. The creature turned its head and looked at Amy. She looked into those mysterious green eyes and suddenly a picture of herself petting its neck appeared in her mind. Amy thought this had to be the result of the Baby Zapatsaur's fluids having influenced its mental abilities. She didn't know how but somehow it had automatically opened up her mind to accept telepathic messages. Both the Wizard and Amy could send a telepathic suggestion, but nothing more. Their telepathic ability was determined by the evolution of their race. Amy sent a suggestion of her petting the creature.

So, she quickly concluded that this was an adolescent creature offering a simple friendly introduction.

"I'd like you to meet a new member of our family." The Wizard said.

"Believe it or not, we've already introduced ourselves." Amy said to a surprised Wizard.

Amy walked over to the creature and began stroking its neck.

"Our new family member is a very beautiful creature." Amy said.

The Wizard was smiling for two reasons; because he somehow knew that Amy would fall in love with the creature and the nights successful mission.

Sam walked into the room and explained how the plan went well without Heather, Leif or the sentry catching sight of the castle's newest resident. Then he offered to warm up the left-over prime rib roast for the creature and himself. He walked into the kitchen to start the oven. Sam was hungry and decided to warm up the left-over pheasant breasts as well.

The night was drawing to a close. While Sam prepared another feast, Amy and the Wizard were getting more acquainted with the creature.

The Portuguese Captain and crew had all survived and were rowing away to a small island where they could eventually be rescued. They had taken turns rowing as much to stay warm as arrive at their destination quicker. The Captain told his crew that many a sailor had been confined to the hospital for stories about giant squid destroying sailing vessels. Other misfortunate sailors had been accused of selling the ship and were thrown into jail for theft. So, they decided that they would tell a story about battling pirates and narrowly escaping with their lives. They would all agree to be silent about what had really happened. However, in another hundred years people would learn that one of the crew strayed from this plan.

CHAPTER 8

The next morning the sun climbed into a rich blue sky without a cloud in sight. Sally had already been up feeding Heather's Zapatsaur when Mitch and General Zen joined her on the main deck.

"Good morning." Mitch called out. Sally turned and smiled."Good morning Dad. Good morning General." She replied.

"Have you checked the belt. Has it increased in pulses per minute." The General asked.

"It has as a matter of fact. The belt is up to eight pulses per minute." Sally answered.

"I would expect that the Zapatsaur can pick up Heather's thoughts." The General suggested.

"That's a good point General. But how could we ask the Zapatsaur where she is being kept." Mitch asked.

"The Zapatsaur may not be able to tell us precise details but it will, as of now, already know the kind of information we need to know in order to formulate a plan for rescue. I think I have an idea." Sally said. Sally walked across to a door on the main deck and entered the cabin. She returned carrying a picture in a frame that was painted by a talented Azorkan artist. The painting was ahead and shoulders portrait of Heather. Sally walked back over to Heather's Zapatsaur and placed the picture on the deck close enough for the Zapatsaur to see it. Sally straightened up then stroked the Zapatsaur's neck and looked into the creature's reptilian eyes.

"If you can hear Heather's thoughts, please place your right foot close to the picture. If you cannot hear Heather's thoughts then move your left foot back." Sally instructed.

The Zapatsaur moved its right foot forward."Fantastic." General Zen said.

Sally thought for a moment. Heather would know that by now her Zapatsaur was close. She activated the device but she wouldn't want to put her Zapatsaur in harm's way. She would select a time for when it could safely rescue her. Heather would know when the enemy was relaxed and not on their guard.

Sally remembered that she had a sundial aboard her ship from the last brief voyage in the ship three weeks ago.

"Wait a second. I'll be right back." Sally shouted out to Mitch and General Zen.

She ran up the stairs for the upper deck two at a time. After a quick moment they heard a door slam and Sally came bounding back down the stairs, landing on the main deck with a thump. Tucked under her arm was the wooden sundial. It was artistically crafted from circassian walnut and polished to a high gloss. The dial was made of gold. Tamara had given it to her as a family heirloom from Siberia.

Sally placed the sundial in front of Heather's Zapatsaur then stood back and addressed the creature."When the sun is halfway through the day the sundial will be at this position." Sally said.

She pointed to that position on the sundial for the Zapatsaur to see.

"When the sun goes down and it becomes dark, the sundial will be on this last position." Sally said. Again, she pointed to the position.

Looking directly into the eyes of Heather's Zapatsaur, Sally asked her question.

"When will you leave to rescue Heather." Sally asked.

The Zapatsaur pointed to the last position. Sally reached up and stroked its neck signaling the end of the questions and her appreciation for its participation.

Sally returned her attention to a surprised Mitch and General Zen who had watched the whole process with a growing sense of amazement.

"General, I must thank you for sharing with me the communication by diagram that you experienced at the Zapatsaur's mountain home. It will be our future challenge to develop a pictorial alphabet. The exercise confirms that Heather's rescue has been organized by her own assumption that the Zapatsaur would pick up her thoughts when within a fifty-mile distance from her. She must have guessed correctly the time it would take the Zapatsaur to reach that distance then repeated the instructions over and over in her mind like sending out a beacon. We don't know where she is but the Zapatsaur does. I would say she is being held in the castle. The castle is a big place and we need to know where. One of us has to stay here as a back up to follow behind with a laser rifle when Heather's Zapatsaur departs to carry out the rescue mission. We should be prepared for any possibility involving the fire breathing creatures or Dragon Queen in case she's not in her cave." Sally finished.

"I'll stay behind and follow out with the Zapatsaur." the General volunteered.

The General thought Sally and Mitch capable of capturing the Dragon Queen without his assistance. One well-placed shot with the tranquilizing arrow would guarantee that the Dragon Queen would remain unconscious for twelve hours. She was not heavy or bulky so Mitch should be able to carry her back in the net on his own Zapatsaur. If Mitch missed with his arrow then Sally would fire hers. Either way the Dragon Queen's incredible strength would not foil the capture while she was unconscious. They would both fly back to the ship and chain the Dragon Queen to the platform in the ship's hold.

Mitch said,"If we set out in another seven hours, that should give us an extra hour of preparation before the Dragon Queen will be leaving her cave to do a little hunting for her dinner. If she doesn't leave when expected, Sally can bait her to come out and then well hit her."

"I would agree with that." Sally said.

"Then I'll go and double check to be sure we have the ship's hold ready for the Dragon Queen. I have to be sure those chains are secure enough to hold her. If not, we will hit her with an arrow so she stays unconscious long enough to get her back to Azorka." Mitch said.

Sally left the main deck returning to her cabin on the top deck, as Mitch walked towards the hatch for the ships hold. Heather's Zapatsaur was looking down at the picture of Heather. Zen leaned on the ships rail and looked out across the water in the direction of the Wizard's castle which was about ten miles away.

There was a silence on board the ship which felt peaceful. All that could be heard was the ocean splashing up against the ship on a beautiful sunny day. A gentle morning breeze ruffled the General's white shirt and a distant seagull sang its morning song. The feeling of a lull before a storm the General thought.

Sam and Leif had enjoyed the sunrise as they finished the final preparations before setting sail on their voyage to Haiti. The Wizard had congratulated them on a job well done. Then he said that there were more rumors of the locations for other crystal skulls around the world. Some had said that his bronze colored crystal skull had been seen in Peru. The Wizard was hoping for more information. He suggested that if the situation allowed for socializing with the local folk, who may have heard such rumors, please take time to do so and see what you can find out. But for now, when you recover the crystal skull, return as soon as possible.

Sam and Leif had assured the Wizard of the mission's success then the two-set sail while the sun was still rising in the sky. Captain Sam commanded the Empire's ship and Captain Leif the lion commanded his own. They were alone on the ocean and soon became a couple of barely discernable specs on the southern horizon, sailing towards their destination unaware of the challenges that awaited them.

The Wizard had hurried back to the castle to see how his creature was doing and to be sure that breakfast was prepared for Heather. He arrived to find his creature was not feeling well. Amy was with the creature stroking its neck in a vain attempt to comfort it. She had placed a blanket over it because the creature was complaining about chills. The Wizard bent down and examined its eyes. He noticed an extra fold of skin under both eyes that wasn't there last night.

"I'm sorry you don't feel well my friend. Amy and I will take care of you. Please just rest while Amy and I prepare breakfast for our guest." The Wizard said.

He spoke out loud in a soothing voice. The Wizard thought his creature may have caught a cold or virus. Maybe the extra fold of skin under each eye was a reptilian reaction to the virus. He didn't think the prime rib roast they fed it last night would produce this kind of complication. He made a note to carefully watch the progress of the virus so that he could make the best decision on how to treat it.

As the Wizard stood back up he received two letters in his mind which startled him."O and K" were the two letters. Had the creature somehow learned the English language overnight.

He looked down in his astonishment at the creature and silently asked, knowing that it must be able to read his mind,"Can you read and write in our language now."

The creature's eyes slowly blinked. It was so drained of energy.

"Yes, I can Wizard. I have read and stored the thoughts of Sam and Amy as well as yourself, so that! could learn your language quickly. However, I fear that my ability to learn quickly and mature quickly may be abnormal development for me. Perhaps I have aged to soon. I need to sleep now." The creature replied telepathically.

The communication had been sent telepathically into the Wizard's mind except"abnormal development" which appeared in print for emphasis. It was a respectful suggestion to revise his experiments so that his future creatures could mature at a slower rate.

The Wizard bent down and pet his creature gently on the head and silently reassured it he would find a solution for its current condition but for now rest would be the best remedy. He rose and turning to Amy he signaled her with a wave of his hand to follow him into the kitchen. He would keep his telepathic messages from his creature to himself so he wouldn't alarm Amy who had become quite fond of the creature. The Wizard was also developing his own feelings for the creature. With the suspicion of premature old age affecting the creature, he was very concerned for its survival.

Inside the kitchen, the Wizard spoke softly.

"We need a quick breakfast for Heather. I have to finish off the experiment today and I'm curious, actually excited about what may be revealed. I need you to hang some tapestry over the creature so that it will be hidden from Heather."

"I can have bacon and eggs with brown toast ready in no time followed by some of our island's pears and yogurt." Amy said.

"Thank you, Amy, that sounds great. I'll head over to the tower and wake Heather."

He hurried out of the room. Amy selected a tapestry and hung it over the alcove in the wall which hid the creature from view.

Outside the bright daylight sent mild pin pricks of pain into the Wizard's eyes. He had spent to many hours underground which had sensitized his eyes. The Wizard arrived at the tower grateful for its dimly lit interior and climbed the stairs to Heather's room. Before he could reach the last six stairs Heather came out of her room and with a big smile she looked down at the Wizard.

"I'm starved. I waited until I saw you coming along the path and decided to walk down to meet you. It looks like you beat me to it. Sorry I wanted to save you the effort of climbing the stairs." Heather said.

"Why thank you for your consideration. I know Amy has a fantastic breakfast waiting for us, so I'm glad you're hungry." The Wizard replied with a smile.

He turned and led the way down the stairs. Outside a couple of crows were squawking and fighting over a small crust of bread. They must have snatched it from the kitchen window where the loaf of bread was put to cool down after being pulled from the oven.

Inside the reception room, the dining table was set for three. Heather took the same chair she had sat in yesterday, and Amy sat across from her facing the tapestry which hid the creature. The Wizard was the last to sit down and he faced the entrance to the orange marble hallway. The hungry trio filled their plates with bacon and eggs and the freshly baked brown bread. Heather could understand why the crows were fighting for the crust. This was the most delicious bread she had ever tasted.

"I think we can finish the experiment this morning. There's not much left to do." The Wizard said. He buttered his brown toast then dipped it into egg yolk.

"Sounds good to me Wizard." Heather replied.

She knew this would be the last session because if all went as planned, if her Zapatsaur has heard her message, she'd be leaving tonight.

Heather was certain that her very limited knowledge and involvement in Azorka's secret affairs made her a poor candidate for the Wizard if the results were intended to gain an advantage for evil purposes. If the Wizard wanted to give the coordinates to the sunken Aryan factory as a goodwill offer for Azorka, then she would be happy about participating. There was nothing of a military nature that Heather was made privy to except the locator belt wrapped around her Zapatsaur and the Wizard hadn't stumbled onto it or the special switch on her control console. With any luck, her Zapatsaur would continue to hear her message that she repeated periodically in her mind. This would be her ride out tonight.

Amy was quiet during breakfast. Her thoughts were centered on the creature's condition and she was at little worried. After fifteen minutes the morning meal concluded with Amy getting up and clearing the table while Heather and the Wizard left to complete the experiment in the Wizard's office.

"Amy, thanks for a fantastic breakfast. I'll return in the afternoon and we'll continue the lessons for swordplay." Heather called out.

Amy turned her head on the way into the kitchen to answer but Heather had already disappeared through the door which led to the office and her hidden room.

Heather climbed the stairs following the Wizard into his office. He pulled the gold drapes on a sunny day until he got the lighting necessary for hypnosis. Heather placed the helmet on her head then looked at the crystal the Wizard was dangling in front of her, swinging it back and forth, six-inches from her eyes. After a few minutes and the count backwards, which sent Heather back in time ten-thousand years ago, the second experiment was fully launched. Heather was going back to recall from genetic memory the actions of her ancestor Julia. Heather would see through the eyes of Julia, a Guardian with the responsibility of inspecting the facility used for Firestone maintenance. And what she saw was valuable information for the Wizard.

The Wizard waited for the imagery to appear on his screen while Heather stared blankly ahead completely void of any facial expression. Julia appeared on the screen, a lone pilot, in a small tear-drop shaped flying machine. The flying machine was about twelve-feet wide, ten-feet long and tapered down. to a width of five-feet in the back. Julia looked down at the wide dash board and the various gauges and screens that helped her navigate, adjust for the speed of the craft, record the temperature of the craft and its crystal energy levels. She held a throttle in her right hand to steer and accelerate or decelerate. She was currently traveling at three hundred miles per hour. She had a relaxed grip on the throttle and flew four-feet above a long and flat field. The shadow cast from the flying machine blazed over the high green grass of summer. After a short moment, Julia was gliding past installations, and had cut her speed down to one-hundred miles per hour. She flew past buildings and factories situated in south Azorka and looked from side to side, through the glass of the flying machine. The Wizard could see that she was heading back to the facility for Firestone maintenance. Julia's craft began to slow down as she approached the facility. She brought her flying machine to a stop fifty-yards from the facility and hovered four-feet above the ground while she looked around the area. She had an unobstructed view looking through the three-foot high resilient glass that covered the top and rounded to the contours of the polished grey metal half of the craft.

Julia looked at the facilities tower, the top of which now housed the Firestone. She unfolded a portable telescope, and saw the tools and additional machinery added for work currently underway. Julia quickly folded up her telescope returning it to a pocket in her white robe. She was extremely upset, her expression a mask of anxiety and fear as she swung her flying machine around to return to north Azorka. She accelerated to two-hundred miles per hour in about ten seconds flying ninety-feet over the domed buildings and smaller pyramids of the south's villages and installations. The work currently underway on the south's Firestone, the special machinery in place, led Julia to believe that the rebels were weaponizing the Firestone.

Julia was rushing back to tell her military commanders of the danger. She arrived back on the long green field again and accelerated to five-hundred miles per hour, flying six-feet above the surface.

The Wizard had the location of the facility now and quite possibly this was the Firestone's last stop before war broke out. It would no longer find its home in a pyramid built over magnetic ley lines in this day and age. Since the flood, the magnetic ley lines had become useless because the Earth's axial rotation was altered, so some theories claimed. The Wizard didn't care, he wanted the Firestone's power as a weapon against the outside world, should they fail to meet his demands. He was about to get up and conclude the experiment because he had all the information he was after, when suddenly a laser bolt hit Julia's craft, sending it spiraling out of control. Julia fought bravely at the controls to regain stable flight but lost the struggle and crashed into an embankment on the edge of what is now Azorka's southern tip of the island Kingdom. The crash sent up a huge ball of flame into the sky.

Heather began screaming and patting her face with her hands as though trying to put out a fire. The Wizard rushed over quick as he could and removed Heather's helmet then snapped his fingers by her ears which brought her mind back to the present. For the first time in an hour he saw her eyes blinking rapidly as she began to come around.

"Do you remember anything?" He asked.

"How long was I under?" Heather asked.

"About one hour. Do you remember anything?" The Wizard persisted.

"Nothing. I remember putting on the helmet and watching the crystal move back and forth. Then I was counting backwards from one-hundred and that's when I lose my recollection." Heather answered. The Wizard raised one of his bushy grey eyebrows and brushed back his pointy grey hat in surprise. He wondered if the memories of the experiment would remain submerged in her subconscious. Would the memory of Julia's tragedy resurface at a later date? Then she may realize the deception and know that she had actually been helping to locate the Empire's Firestone. The Wizard decided he would worry about that when or if it happens.

"Well the experiment was a success and I have the coordinates for the Aryan factory which I'll record and send with you when you leave in a couple of days." The Wizard said.

The Wizard reached down offering Heather his hand to help her up. She got up and felt a little dizzy but was still in good health. They left the office and went back downstairs. Amy had moved the creature out of the reception room while Heather was upstairs with the Wizard. The tapestry still hid the alcove which was being prepared for new bookcases. Amy had thought ower her options for the creature's comfort. She finally found a warm spot in the Wizard's laboratory and moved the creature to it. Amy had placed a few warm blankets over top of the shivering creature with its drooping eyes then sent a message that she'd return in a few hours.

In the reception room, the morning dishes had been cleared off the dining room table and Amy walked into the room carrying a floral arrangement and placed it in the center of the table. She looked over at the Wizard who had entered the room after walking Heather to her room, so she could rest. He returned her gaze with a comforting smile.

"I trust that all has been cleared, moved and secured." He paused"I thank you Amy." The Wizard knew that if anything was wrong, that she would usher him into the kitchen, out of the range of other ears and explain the predicament.

"Everything is done kind Wizard." Amy replied with a smile.

"I understand Heather is teaching you sword-play. That is great exercise and a useful skill in this day and age. I thought I would leave you both briefly in order to attend to some chores of my own."

The Wizard returned to his office and began going over his notes from the recent experiment. Julia's instruments were lit up a bright green on her dashboard in the flying machine so it was easy for the Wizard to record the date and the time of the event. It was six hours before the outbreak of the final chapter of this war and twelve hours until all this land and technology fell to the bottom of the ocean. Julia had been hit with a laser bolt from the south's Firestone while it was in the facility. The south's security had caught on to Julia and took her down for what she had witnessed. This signaled the beginning of the end. The Wizard wrote down the longitude and latitude for the Firestone on his papyrus note pad.

On a separate piece of his note pad he wrote some phony coordinates down for the Aryan factory just one mile south of Azorka. This he would give to Heather when he sets her free in a couple of days. There was still more information he wanted from Heather which would help him combat his opponents in Azorka.

The Wizard stopped writing and got up from his desk, walked over to the large window and opened the drapes. His north westerly view revealed a descending sun which would gradually be turning red. The day would be over in another couple of hours.

The Wizard gave a sigh at the thought of all the hard work and trouble he had gone through for thousands of years now in order to gain control of this planet. Amy his most faithful friend and fellow scientist from his world, had been there to help every step of the way. Should he have to go off planet on a short mission, she would rule in his place. Once all was accomplished and all safeguards in place, including the destruction of that Yetz satellite that shot down his craft all those years ago, The Wizard would make Amy Queen over this world then depart leaving her in charge. The Wizard had other missions to complete in this solar system, then a new weapon to overcome those forces ruling on his home planet, which will be a beneficial invasion for his allies in other solar systems.

In order to accomplish this, he required the assistance he would receive from all thirteen of his crystal skulls when they were found. Each crystal skull, built by the Wizard, with the assistance of his allies" equipment, became a living entity when the Wizard's craft was applied to the crystal. The crystal skulls are extremely sensitive to ultra violet rays from this solar system. Inside the crystal skull, various indentations had been lasered inside of the quartz material with specialized laser tools. Those indentations produce a working brain, filled to the brim with all the information of the universe. When all thirteen are assembled as the perfect team, feeding off each other's specialized knowledge, they can problem solve and provide a timely solution to any problem.

The Wizard gazed out his window towards the field on his left. It had that seasonal brown color and it was where his forty-foot fire breathing flying creature had returned to its pen for rest. A special glass dome, darkened to keep out sunlight, slid over the pen and automatically locked to keep the creature in. But soon now the creature would be growling to get out. The enormous pen for this creature was two-hundred yards from the beach and concealed sixty-feet below the surface. If the Wizard pressed a button on his control console which he kept in his desk, the dome would slide open releasing the fire-breathing monster. The Wizard felt ready for any future challenge to his Kingdom. He was also a little nervous about having Heather here longer than he expected, and the possibility of retaliation.

The afternoon had about another hour to go before sunset. Mitch and Sally had flown off towards the Dragon Queen's cave located in the highest of the peaks for the rock cliffs sheltering the castle. They used the bright rays from the setting sun to conceal their approach flying four feet from the ocean surface. They reached the Dragon Queen's cliff and found cover at the base of it under a large overhang of rock, the result of erosion due to the marine process. The two Zapatsaurs, Mitch and Sally huddled together underneath. They would wait another half hour before Sally appeared at the cave entrance and Mitch about twenty-feet below her ready to shoot and retrieve the unconscious Dragon Queen's falling body with the net. This being the revised plan, they had come up with. Sally looked out in the direction they had flown from. Now the ship was only five-miles away and awaiting the successful completion of both missions. Soon Heather's Zapatsaur would depart on its mission of rescue with the General flying behind as back up with a laser rifle. This was a critical time. They had to be quick about the Dragon Queen's capture in case Heather's escape didn't go smoothly.

The ship was distant enough to be out of sight from the Empire. General Zen and his Zapatsaur were on the main deck and ready to follow behind when Heather's Zapatsaur decided to leave. All was quiet except the sounds from the ocean and occasionally a shout from one of the crew members.

The setting sun was polishing a calm ocean red and the arriving evening was ready to drop its curtain over lingering rays of sun. Quiet and picturesque except for the flashing of light reflecting off a metallic and strange looking object traveling just five-feet above the ocean surface heading straight for the ship. The General looked on in amazement as the metallic, tear-drop shaped flying craft rose up to six feet above the port side rail and landed ten-feet away from the General and the Zapatsaurs. The Zapatsaurs remained calm detecting no danger from the visitor. The top half of the flying machine was covered in glass which molded to the curved contours of the polished metal base. A glass hatch above the pilot opened out and Lana, Heather's best friend, hopped down onto the deck as the ship's engine shut down making a peculiar mechanical whining sound.

"I've come to help my friend escape. I have permission from the deputy commander. I was able to prove the capabilities of this flying machine and how it may be of assistance in the rescue. This will be the first time in ten-thousand years that the Aryans have regained the art of flight and we're proud of this achievement." Lana said.

She had a deeper voice than Sally or Heather and was about six-feet tall with bright blonde hair, almost yellow. It shone like gold in the setting sun, was bound with a dark headband and fell past her shoulders in length. Lana's eyes were a sky-blue color, with black pupils that were rectangular albeit with rounded corners. This was a genetic trait that was gradually fading. Hundreds of thousands of years ago this was the shape for all of the Aryan's pupils, but today Lana was the only person with these pupils in the Aryan village ten miles south east of the Zapatsaur's mountain.

"I'm glad to see you Lana. Our military branch was made aware of your recent success and reported it to me just before I left on this mission. But I didn't expect you folks to risk the craft in this mission." The General said.

"This is my best friend we're talking about. The flying craft is equipped with a laser cannon that is mounted on a swivel for multiple direction selection. The outside is a fire proof metal and the glass dome are capable of resisting extreme heat and flame. It's designed to take down the Wizard's flying horrors. The flying machine is agile, maneuverable and quick. It can fly as fast as three hundred miles per hour, so far, although this is half the speed of a similar model from ten thousand years ago. It will seat a second person behind me, another design change from the original which sat two occupants' side by side." Lana finished.

The General gave a smile and thumbs up then he took about twenty minutes to fill Lana in on all that had gone on in the last forty-eight hours. He suggested that she ride high in the sky as a back up to the mission they were about to leave on and he told her his plan.

"So, when you see Heather's Zapatsaur leave we do the same and follow a slight distance behind." The General said.

"Got it." Lana said.

She climbed back into her flying craft, seated herself and pulled the crisscross seatbelt over her white robe and fastened it. She sat there watching Heather's Zapatsaur while the General returned to stand beside his Zapatsaur.

Heather's Zapatsaur must have had its own method of measuring time. Sally had cleared away the picture of Heather and the sun-dial, believing them no longer necessary for the Zapatsaur, before she left with Mitch to capture the Dragon Queen. She had been correct. Suddenly Heather's Zapatsaur started to walk forward on the deck in order to clear the sail above then sprung into the night, its leathery wings flapping rapidly as it disappeared from sight.

The General waited a short moment then mounted his Zapatsaur and took off into the night following behind. Lana was, as planned, the last to leave. She slowly did her lift-off from the deck and gave a quick wave to the few crew members who had gathered to watch the flying machine leave. They were extremely interested in this new technology the Aryan's had brought back to life. The flying craft hovered slowly above the ocean then turned and sped off through the night sky.

Lana flew up high in the night sky and turned on her scanner which was on the dashboard. The scanner was equipped with a night vision lens so she could see both Zapatsaurs clearly as they flew four feet above the ocean surface traveling beside the light from the moon. General Zen's Zapatsaur was keeping a distance of two hundred yards behind Heather's Zapatsaur.

Back under the overhang on the Dragon Queen's cliff face, Sally and Mitch walked their Zapatsaurs back outside at the base of the cliff then mounted and flew up the cliff face slowly trying to stay in the shadows that boulders and ledges provided. Mitch had his quiver full of the newly developed copper tranquilizing arrow the military had produced. He checked his belt and released the strap for his sword just in case of unexpected resistance from the Dragon Queen. The net he had packed was in front of him. Mitch was ready for a special maneuver he had practiced with his Zapatsaur. He was amongst the few in the Kingdom strong enough to capture the Dragon Queen's unconscious bulk in a net.

Sally released the latch for her sword to be sure it was ready to be drawn. This is the weapon she will use to challenge the Dragon Queen. She checked her bow, pulling back on the string and loading it with a tranquilizing arrow then locking it in place. Sally looked upward as they flew closer to the Dragon Queen's cave in the cliff's upper face. She looked down a few yards to where Mitch was following close behind and silently signaled him pointing upwards at the cave entrance now seventy-yards away. Mitch gave a thumbs up in acknowledgement. In another minute, Sally was within twenty-yards of the entrance and again she looked down at Mitch signaling with her hands for him to get into position. She hovered just below the cave entrance and watched Mitch prepare for the kill shot. Mitch was kneeling on his Zapatsaur's back while it hovered ten-feet below Sally's position. He drew the arrow from his quiver and placed it in his bow. Now he was ready for the shot. Sally rose up the remaining twenty-yards. and began yelling for the Dragon Queen at the cave entrance.

CHAPTER 9

Lana was five-thousand feet above the Empire's island and using the telescopic lens for the scanner. She was watching the General and Heather's Zapatsaur take a route to the castle through the forest and over rock strewn hills. They were about one-hundred yards apart now as they arrived around the hill that sheltered the castle. They were using an approach opposite to the approach Mitch and Tamara had taken earlier, a strategy that Heather's Zapatsaur had already picked up on. The General would have to creep around the hill's rock base and take flight when the moment was right. This felt like a test of the General's nerves because from this point forward, only Heather's Zapatsaur knew the game plan and he would have to wait and see what it would do before moving himself. He was glad to have Lana looking in as extra backup.

In the tower Heather had written a note for Amy and the Wizard thanking them for their hospitality and promising to take the Wizard's message of peace and cooperation back to Azorka. Heather also asked that they forgive her abrupt departure and broken window frame. She got up from the small desk leaving the note in place and walked over to the window and kicked out the decorative wooden bars. She got up on the window ledge ready to jump.

The General was beginning to perspire from his anxiety when he heard the crack of wood echo from the surrounding cliffs behind the castle's tower. Immediately Heather's Zapatsaur bolted for that direction flying fast fifteen-feet above the ground. The General followed, his Zapatsaur flying behind by about fifty-yards. The General stopped in the shadow of a tree and hovered there while he watched the rescue. Heather's Zapatsaur had reached the tower and was hovering four-feet below, what he assumed to be Heather's window. The General checked his laser rifle he had strapped to his back. He would be ready if the sudden appearance of the Wizard's flying creatures threatened their rescue. Suddenly the General saw Heather step outside onto her window ledge and drop from the window landing on the back of her Zapatsaur four-feet below. Her Zapatsaur took off flying around the back of the tower then swiftly over to the General. Heather looked over at the General with a welcome expression while they both hovered in the shadow of the large tree.

"It's good to see you Zen and thank you. I'll let you lead us out of here." Heather whispered.

The General gave a quick nod of his head and without a word led the way, flying back around the rock base of the hill. Both Zapatsaur's were familiar with the route they had taken earlier so the General urged his Zapatsaur to maximum speed.

Heather and the General flew over fields and rock-strewn hills. Then they reached the forest. Heather hung on for dear life, absolutely amazed that her Zapatsaur could fly at such a high-speed weaving in and out of trees in its path. They must have been flying at sixty-miles per hour and she wondered about her Zapatsaur's eye sight. It must have incredible eye sight and reflexes to fly at this speed through a natural obstacle course only five-feet off the ground. They slowed down then stopped as they arrived at the forest edge, which bordered an open field. They were just three-hundred yards away from the beach.

The Wizard had heard the echo of the sharp crack of wood coming from outside. He got up from his desk and went to the window just in time to see two riders on Zapatsaurs disappear around a rocky out crop. They were fleeing shadows in the night, but the Wizard had caught a flash of Heather's white robe and long hair blowing behind her in the moonlight. He raced over to his desk and pressed the button on his control console which would free his forty-foot long fire breathing creature.

He walked back over to the window to watch the release of his creature sixty-feet below the dome and one-hundred yards from the beach. In a couple of minutes, the dome had slid into the recess cut in the earth. With a horrible scream, which echoed off the surrounding hillside, the Wizard's creature rose into the cold night air. Its ten-foot long scaly black neck supported a head somewhat similar to a crocodile. Yellow and red eyes burned like two hideous lanterns in the night. A twenty-foot long black scaly body had two arms and two legs which were covered in black scaly segments and well-developed muscle. The ten-foot long tail swept back and forth in the night sky as it turned from side to side, looking for an enemy, while it hovered above the pen. Suddenly it stopped its scanning and looked in the direction of the forest's edge. The creature's fifteen-foot leathery wings started pumping up and down quicker and it started out in the direction of the forests edge to investigate.

The Wizard's view from the window ended quickly as the creature raced down the field. He assumed the creature had caught sight of the rescue party emerging from the forest. His creature would destroy both Zapatsaurs and riders in a lethal ball of flame.

Lana had seen the entire escape on her scanner. It was perfectly executed with Heather jumping out of the tower's window on to her Zapatsaur. The General was there to guide her back and it was like watching a race they flew so fast over hills and through the forest. She wished she could have flown behind Heather to test her flying craft for agility. It looked as though Heather and Zen had escaped unnoticed until the problem appeared. Lana knew that this was what the General's anxiety was all about; the Wizard's fire breathing creatures. This ugly horror was hovering in mid-air and looking at Heather and the General as though trying to decide when to attack. The General was slowly bringing his laser rifle around which swiveled into place by a strap around his shoulder. The creature was getting ready to attack.

Lana knew she could fly circles around the creature and she had an opportunity to test the laser cannon in combat. She quickly dropped the nose of her flying craft to a sixty-degree angle and accelerated. The ground was rushing up at her and in the next second, she decided to fire the laser cannon. The field, no more than three-feet in front of the creature, exploded in a fiery starburst with startling effect. The creature, no longer interested in Heather and Zen, quickly turned its ugly neck and head and shot a stream of fire at Lana as she, without fear flew through it in her fire-resistant craft. The creature leaped into the dark sky and began chasing after the flying craft. Lana decided to fly upwards at the same sixty-degree angle she had descended on. She would let the creature get close then accelerate swiftly upwards and fly over the creature to come up behind the monster for the kill shot. But first she would tire it out a little. Lana suddenly changed course and sped downwards on a forty-five-degree angle with the creature flying fiercely after her. Lana changed direction again flying upwards with the creature howling its frustration and flying after her. Lana let it get closer, from a height of about one-hundred feet then quickly accelerated and looped upwards, flying upside down briefly over the creature and recovering right side up and behind the creature. Lana shot the creature three times with her laser cannon. The laser charges connected with both wings and the creature's back. The craft's technology was working perfectly. The Wizard's creature exploded in mid-air and most of its destroyed body parts landed with a colossal thump in the field fifty-yards from its pen.

Lana was pleased with her flying craft's combat abilities. Fortunately, she did realize that this was not the intelligent version of the Wizard's creatures, so Lana was not over confident because of her success. She realized that in the future there would be a need for a second laser cannon to be installed in the craft. There's a variety of different strategies an intelligent creature could use to challenge a flying craft in combat and combat strategies was a subject she had studied. The Aryan library documented this subject from the war. The battles between the Wizard's creatures and Aryan flying machines built for combat was very detailed.

Lana looked at her scanner's screen on her dashboard and applied the telescopic lens. Looking in the direction of the forest's edge, she saw a cautious General Zen and Heather glancing around in all directions as they flew out to meet her while she hovered fifty-feet above the field. The General arrived first on her side of the craft and hovered in place. He opened his arms wide in a gesture of welcomed relief and bowed his head with gratitude for rescuing them from this horror. Zen, while looking at Lana's flying machine, gave her the thumbs up, as a silent approval of the Aryan's technology.

Next to arrive was Heather on the other side of her flying craft. She just about fell off her Zapatsaur when she looked through the glass of the flying machine and realized that her best friend had rescued them. Heather blew kisses of appreciation as Lana stared out through the craft's glass dome and smilled back, her mysterious blue eyes twinkling in the moonlight. She looked out again at General Zen who was signaling that they should return to the ship and all three, with Lana flying slowly in the middle flew back to Sally's ship.

Sally was hovering at the entrance to the Dragon Queen's cave and swinging her sword in the air while shouting insults into the cave and challenging the evil abomination to a fight.

"Come out of the cave you evil coward." Sally yelled.

Mitch was about twenty-yards below her waiting to shoot the Dragon Queen as soon as she emerged. This would be the toughest shot of the mission. The Dragon Queen was as dangerous as a venomous snake and could strike just as fast. He knew that if he missed and she was free to attack that the lethal claws on her wings end could strike him a fatal blow. She would kill him first then capture Sally for interrogation.

Mitch knew he had to be twenty-yards below her falling mass in order that both Zapatsaur and rider had time to react and synchronize for the catch. Mitch had to lead his shot to compensate for the Dragon Queen's lightning speed and the distance between his target. He aimed for a spot just three-feet away from Sally's Zapatsaur. Mitch figured he would strike either the lower or upper part of the Dragon Queen's torso depending upon her speed and his reaction time.

Inside the cave, the Dragon Queen had moved up to the entrance in order to see what all the noise was about. When she saw who was outside waiting for her, she couldn't believe her luck. Right there in front of her was the prize she had recommended kidnapping and bringing back, yet the Wizard had insisted on Heather. Sally was more knowledgeable about Azorka's secrets. She wouldn't have to be regressed thousands of years backwards in time during a session of hypnotism for the Wizard to uncover information.

The Dragon Queen didn't think further. She couldn't resist the temptation and launched straight out of her cave at Sally with the lightning speed of a reptile about to strike its prey. The distance between Sally and the Dragon Queen had granted just enough reaction time for Sally to reach around for her bow. But it wasn't necessary, as Mitch's arrow had lodged in the Dragon Queen's lower torso only two feet away from contact with Sally's Zapatsaur bravely hovering in place.

Sally watched the Dragon Queen's powerful white wings fold-up as the unconscious monster began to fall. At the same time Mitch and his Zapatsaur were falling below the Dragon Queen. The Zapatsaur could see through Mitch's eyes using its telepathy which allowed it to calculate their distance between the Dragon Queen's body and the net that Mitch was holding high to catch her. Mitch caught the Dragon Queen's unconscious body and closed the net around her bulk, moving along his Zapatsaur's back to make room for the extra passenger. Mitch and his Zapatsaur had fallen seventy yards in ten seconds in order to safely catch their new prisoner. They immediately took off back out to sea with a jubilant Sally flying behind at one-hundred miles per hour in order to keep up.

General Zen, Heather and Lana had arrived back on the ship to howls of congratulations from the crew. Lana had parked her flying machine in the same place on the main deck and in the dim light, the crew were milling around it exchanging comments and opinions. They were excited about this breakthrough for Azorka, thanks to the Aryans. Meanwhile the rescue party were in the main deck's cabin sitting at a dining table and enjoying a glass of wine in celebration of the successful mission.

Heather and Lana were sitting side by side facing the window of the small wood paneled room which had a view of Lana's flying machine. The General sat opposite them enjoying the relaxing effects of the wine.

"General, I must thank the research team Ted works with for the locator device. It saved my life." Heather said.

"It was well crafted and performed perfectly in the field and I'll be sure to congratulate Ted's division." The General replied.

Lana, listening quietly to the conversation, looked across the table at the General and with her approving expression decided to add her own observation.

"That is one very clever boyfriend you've got Heather. Do you think he was intuitive by thinking you could be in some kind of danger and suggested you test it so that he wouldn't worry so much about you."? Lana asked.

"That's an interesting thought Lana, although I feel certain we'll never know. Guy's don't admit to anything that could be perceived as a weakness. Ted is more focused on the success of his division's teamwork, and the benefit for Azorka. But I like that and I'm probably all the more in love with him because of this facet of his personality." Heather answered.

At that moment, one of the crewmen came to the window and knocked on the glass.

"General sir, Heather and Lana. You're going to want to see this." He shouted.

The three got up at the same time and Heather opened the door to the main deck. Heather was the first to see Mitch flying at top speed visible in the moonlight at fifty-yards from the ship, holding the captured and unconscious Dragon Queen in front of him on the back of his Zapatsaur. His Zapatsaur pulled up over the ship's rail and slowly descended on to the ship's main deck no more than five-feet in front of General Zen. The General moved swiftly to relieve Mitch of the unconscious bulk of the Dragon Queen so he could dismount. Zen raised the Dragon Queen bundled in the net from the Zapatsaurs back, and with a grunt of exertion he placed her gently on the deck.

Mitch was walking back and forth on the deck to help with the circulation to some of his cramped muscles, and releasing some of his anxiety.

Finally, Mitch stopped his pacing and turned around to face his friends and family."I'm so relieved that the capture went well. If my shot had been one second slower, it could have been messy." Mitch said.

"You were awesome Dad." Sally said, calling over from the other side of the deck still kneeling on her Zapatsaur's back.

Sally had just arrived. She had seen Lana's flying machine from above and decided to land on that side. Sally got off her Zapatsaur and walked over to join everybody now focused on the sleeping Dragon Queen. Sally looked over at Lana and smiled.

"Lana. It's great to see you. Thank you for joining the rescue party." Sally said.

Then she looked over at her sister and with a joyful expression she ran over and hugged her. Mitch followed and did the same.

After everyone had released their tension and joy, Mitch walked over to the Dragon Queen still wrapped in the net, and raised her up over his shoulder carrying her over to the hatchway for the ships hold. Before Zen could catch up to help Mitch had already disappeared down the stairs to the platform that would hold the Dragon Queen in place securely for the return trip. General Zen walked down the stairs just in time to see Mitch attach the last chain to the Dragon Queen's wrist. She lay there unconscious chained down by her ankles and wrists.

"I don't think she'll be going anywhere if she regains consciousness." The General said.

Mitch looked up as he heard Zen's voice.

"I want to thank you Zen for helping with the rescue of my daughter." Mitch said as he extended his hand to shake the General's.

The General grasped Mitch's hand and shook it."It was my pleasure Mitch." He said.

Mitch started back up the steps to the main deck. He stopped before he reached the top and looked back down at Zen who was about to follow him up.

"I'm going to get that Wizard now. Hopefully, I'll catch him off guard." Mitch said.

Then Mitch turned back and climbed the rest of the steps up and hopped out onto the main deck. By the time Zen climbed out onto the main deck Mitch had already rolled over the laser cannon now pointing in the direction of the Wizard's castle. The cannon was a perfect imitation of a seventeenth century cannon except that it shot a devastating charge of laser energy that could still deliver a destructive charge as far away as twenty-miles. Mitch only had five-miles of distance to adjust the cannon for the kill shot. He looked around and saw that the ladies were in the kitchen of the cabin. A portable crystal lantern attached to the planks of the cabin's roof, lit their animated faces in conversation.

Mitch looked at Zen standing beside him and said,"Cover your ears."

With a large boom that echoed all around and across the ocean surface, Mitch fired the cannon from the starboard side of the ship at the

Wizard's castle. The ladies in the cabin looked out the window to see what had made the noise. They saw Mitch smiling triumphantly maybe more of a mischievous expression.

About twenty minutes before Mitch had fired the laser cannon, the Wizard was in his office standing by the window frozen in a moment of stunned amazement. He thought that he had seen a ghost. His fire breathing creature had been completely destroyed by what looked like an Aryan flying machine. The exact same tear-drop shaped flying machine he had seen only a few short hours ago. The craft would signal a great advancement for Azorka and a challenge to the Wizard's creatures. The only creature he had now that would stand a chance against it was downstairs and either extremely sick or dying. If it was healthy he would be able to outfit his creature with both shield and laser weapon after a few quick lessons. The creature would be smart enough to click the shield off and on in combat when it wanted to fire its weapon. The remainder of the Wizard's creatures would be easily shot out of the sky and destroyed. However, they might stand a chance if they all attacked the flying craft at the same time overwhelming their target by sheer numbers.

Before the Wizard could plan out his strategy he received a picture in his mind. His creature was lying on its side on some pillows in his lab that Amy had brought. The creature looked very sick. The Wizard left his office and walked down the steps to the reception room.

Amy was sitting at the dining table lost in thought. The floral arrangement in front of her seemed to be wilting with her mood. She hadn't put her contacts in and her dark eyes were moist with sadness. Amy looked up as the Wizard walked over to the table.

"I'm afraid our friend is looking so sick that it may die. I don't want to lose my beautiful friend." Amy said choking back tears.

"Our friend was calling me That is why I'm here." The Wizard said. "Let's go and look in on the creature together." He said in a sympathetic tone.

The Wizard led Amy into the laboratory where the creature was laying against the far wall on a bed of cushions and pillows. The Wizard looked at the creature and saw three new folds below the eyes. It looked like old age had arrived early for the creature. The skin was not its usual healthy red but actually looked dull and old. A peculiar odor caught in the Wizard's nostrils and he stood up to avoid the unpleasant smell.

"I'm dying Wizard." The creature was now speaking inside the Wizard's head.

"Now we don't know that for sure." The Wizard said trying to reassure his creature.

"I believe, from what I have studied in your mind, Wizard, that the incompatibility of the various strains of DNA has led to a fatal rapid growth cycle for me. The DNA you brought from your planet and the Zapatsaur DNA, I believe clash when combined. Your experiment with recombinant DNA may need more refining if you are to conquer this effect."

"I thank you for your observations. We still have other options available for keeping you alive." The Wizard said.

"The really positive outcome from your experiment is that somehow this enhanced my telepathy. Now I only have an estimated ten-minutes to live. I'm the equivalent of eighty years old and have decayed as you can see. The Zapatsaurs and humans on average live for the same amount of years. Maybe another strain of off-planet DNA will be the answer to this problem." The creature telepathically replied.

The Wizard was somewhat speechless, not knowing what to say next.

"Your enemies are thinking about firing a laser cannon at the castle. That's another reason I called you. I want you to protect yourself and Amy from harm. I also want to say good bye and thank you for my life and your kindness." The creature finished.

Amy was wiping away tears as the creature's eyes closed. The Wizard felt sadness as well as shock and, in another moment, he swung into action.

"I have to activate the castle's shields." He said.

Then he out of the laboratory and through the reception room. He was huffing and puffing with the exertion by the time he opened the door to the stairs. He bounded up the stairs two at a time and made it into office wheezing like an old man. He ran to the back window again and flicked a switch built into the wall beside the window casing. He opened the window a crack and cool air rushed into his office. Outside the Wizard could hear the hum of the crystal powered generator for the castle's shields. It was a large crystal brilliantly crafted over ten-thousand years ago and very powerful. It had to be in order to cast a huge domed and invisible shield over the castle and its tower. The shield could resist the most powerful laser charges, even up close.

The Wizard relaxed a few moments until, to his surprise, he could see a red flash streaking across the sky. He braced himself for the impact. The red flash, most likely from the laser cannon, was headed straight for the castle. With a loud and horrific explosion, the red laser charge connected with the Wizard's shield. The laser charge broke up violently into a starburst pattern sending shards of red laser energy in all directions. But the castle was not harmed nor was the Wizard's powerful shield weakened.

So, you want to entertain me with your useless toys he thought. I'll send out the remainder of my creatures and will see if there able to overwhelm you before you can destroy them. The Wizard walked over to his desk and pulled the wide but slim drawer directly under the center of the table top. He pulled out a wooden board decorated with color-coded switches that represented the various locations of pens for his creatures on other parts of the island. As soon as he turned on the switch the dome over top of the creature's pen would start to slide open. The creatures were trained to fly to the Wizard's window and receive instructions. The Wizard would point in the direction of the enemy and the creature would fly in that direction to find the enemy it had been trained to kill. The Wizard's creatures were developed with the DNA from his planet mixed with the DNA of some of Earth's most fierce creatures.

Unfortunately, the intellectual result was very limited comprehension and low IQ. The Wizard had trained them to attack anything in the direction his wand was pointing. He took of his cone shaped hat and from an inside strap removed a slender wand no more than four-inches in length. He walked over to the window and opened it wider just as one of his creatures arrived. It was a fire breathing thirty-foot flying lizard with bright orange and yellow scales barely visible in the dim light of night. It hovered in front of the Wizard's window awaiting his command. The lizard's large head moved slightly and moonlight caught a couple rows of razor-sharp teeth. The creature's arms and legs were rippled in muscle and its hands and feet were lethal weapons with eight-inch claws. The Wizard held the slender wand out the window pointing in the direction he estimated, where the ship would be judging by the incoming laser charges. He pressed a small switch on his wand and it shot out a guiding streak of light which pierced the darkness. The creature would destroy anything in the path the Wizard's wand had illuminated and beyond until it was satisfied with the kill and returned home to its pen. The creature that was hovering while waiting for instruction, turned in this direction. Screeching at such a high pitch that the sound bounced around the cliffs sheltering the castle, it flew out to sea at an incredible speed then disappeared from sight.

Sally lit the last of the seven lamps, providing light on the deck. A relaxed Zen, Mitch, Heather and Lana looked on seated on a bench built into the lower deck. The lamp had both clear and amber colored glass providing dimer, but relaxing lighting. The large candle caught and she withdrew her hand closing the glass, Lana's flying machine glowed a bright silver in the light.

Sally was about to sit down and join the group when Lana noticed that something was bothering the Zapatsaurs. They were moving back and forth on the deck and looking out across the ocean in the direction of the Wizard's castle. Lana believed they sensed danger approaching in the night.

"I was worried about retaliation from the Wizard after Mitch had fired those three laser bursts." She said."The Wizard probably has a shield over the castle."

Lana ran to her ship opened the top, climbed over and strapped herself into her seat securely. She closed the top glass which sealed itself to the metal half below. The tear-drop shaped flying machine rose and as Lana activated a switch, a bright stream of light penetrated the darkness. To her absolute horror, not more than one-hundred yards in front of her was the thirty-foot fire breathing lizard. The monster roared with anger from the bright light stinging its eyes. By the time Lana's flying machine had raced upwards in the dark sky to challenge the creature, the monster was no more than fifty-yards away from the ship.

The moonlight was sparkling across those razor-sharp teeth the creature showed Lana and it focused on Lana's craft which hovered in position between the ship and the creature. Lana fired her laser cannon just as the creature released a stream of fire from its angry jaws which had no effect on her fire-proof flying machine. Lana's laser charge reached its target with the precision and accuracy this new technology provided. The lizard's head was blown into three separate chunks which fell into the ocean, the body and lifeless limbs following. Lana looked up and to her surprise ten more of the Wizard's flying horrors in the distance, were flying towards her. Lana realized she would need help with this challenge and began to move her spot light, which swiveled on its own mechanism, back and forth from the ship to the flock of flying monsters the Wizard had released. She continued her warning signal until Mitch began firing his laser cannon into the path of the flying abominations. Immediately two more of the Wizard's creatures were hit by the laser charge and dropped to the ocean, their leathery wings burning as they fell. Mitch fired another volley of laser charge from his cannon. While caught in Lana's light, he noticed that he had hit a rather unusual looking creature about one-hundred yards away. The creature was flying ahead of the remaining pack so Lana could see that Mitch had hit it in the torso. The creature's white wings curled in and it raised its head and howled in pain. It had the head and horns of an elk and two extra arms had powered the white wings which were now curled against its body as it fell to the ocean below. Lana's light caught it again revealing its peculiar blue color. Attached to the heel of those blue feet were two horns eight-inches long. It was still screaming in pain as it splashed through the surface and sank to the bottom of the ocean.

Lana rose higher in the sky while keeping her light on the remaining horde so Mitch could continue firing while she fired down from above. Lana fired off five laser charges and took out three more of the Wizard's creatures at a distance of two-hundred yards. She watched with satisfaction as they dropped into the ocean. Mitch fired off four more laser charges and each one reached its target resulting in four of the Wizard's creatures burning on their way down to the ocean. Lana saw by her spot light that they had killed all of the creatures so she turned her flying machine back to the ship and landed back on the main deck to cheers and clapping.

"You saved the day my dear friend." Heather yelled. She ran up to Lana and hugged her.

"Our position is discovered so let's do whatever it takes to get out of here." Mitch shouted. He called on the crew to set sail right away.

The Wizard had watched from a distance as much as he could see through his telescope and decided he didn't want to see anymore. He knew he had sent all his creatures to their deaths. The Wizard didn't genetically engineer enough intellect for his earlier creations so that they would be able to take evasive action when being fired upon. However, he did need their pens empty for his next generation of creatures. This new breed would be much smarter. But what tipped off his enemies that an attack in the dark was on its way? No doubt the Zapatsaurs had found a way to issue a warning. No other explanation works. The enemy would have been prepared and waiting to devastate the creatures by laser charge sending them burning to the ocean below. Again, the Wizard, a perpetual optimist, looked upon the bright side of past events. This experience would motivate him to make adjustments to his special biology which was not entirely terrestrial. This loss and defeat would never happen again.

The Wizard drew the curtains on the night and left his office to join and cheer up Amy downstairs. She had suffered the loss of a friend. Her next friend will be healthier and live longer, the Wizard vowed.

The next day, during the early afternoon, Sally's ship pulled into Azorka's southern dock. An exhausted crew and Zapatsaurs walked off the ship into a sunny afternoon. There were four Zapatsaurs, sent for relief, already waiting to take the three Guardians and General Zen north to the castle so that the other Zapatsaurs could rest up from the exertion of the mission back in their homes at the Zapatsaur's mountain.

After a quick flight, Zen, Lana and the three Guardians, arrived at the castle. Lana had flown behind the Zapatsaurs and as she touched down to park her flying machine in the front yard, the four Zapatsaurs left returning to their mountain homes.

Mitch had asked some of the military to organize a barbeque meal for the Zapatsaur's entire community. As appreciation for helping the Azorkans during the ordeal. Then Mitch declared a two-day holiday for Azorka to celebrate the capture of the Dragon Queen. She was still unconscious and had been taken to a secured medical facility in village'E'. Here the best medical minds in Azorka could explore the possibilities for rehabilitation and returning her to human form.

Tamara had made everyone a late lunch when they arrived. Relaxation was welcome and felt good after the anxiety of this mission. They sat together at the kitchen table enjoying an after-meal wine that Tamara had opened for the occasion.

"Lana it's always great to see you and thank you for helping with the rescue." Tamara said.

Lana smiled a silent thank you but remained quiet. Sometimes she had a shy side to her personality and would blush slightly from any kind of a compliment. She sat there, her bright blonde hair glowing in the afternoon sun and falling to the shoulders of her white robe. Lana had changed her perspiration-soaked head band for the spare she carried in her flying machine. It wrapped around the top of her head to hold her hair in place, especially when flying. Her blue eyes sparkled, from the skylight in the kitchen. Natural light was collected through an outside glass dome mounted on the exterior wall. The sun's light would travel through a fifteen-foot long shaft built into the ceiling of the kitchen and outfitted with mirrors delivering the sun's rays to the skylight.

Sally glanced across the table at Lana with a look of appreciation and thanks for her efforts. Knowing Heather's best friend as well as she did, Sally avoided a direct compliment.

"General Zen is going to congratulate and thank both Lana's division and Ted's for their contributions to the mission and rescue." Sally said.

"Mitch and I have discussed Sally's idea for a pictorial alphabet for the Zapatsaurs, and we'll be working with Sally to perfect her idea. We also plan to add several more divisions for research and development. Those divisions will be responsible for defensive strategies which will counter attacks by the Wizard." Zen announced.

Mitch was quiet for a moment as he thought over what they had experienced during the mission.

"Heather has told me that the Wizard is seeking his lost crystal skulls. This is a concern to me and possible challenge to both Azorka and the outside world. In the wrong hands and used for destructive purposes, the thirteen skulls can be very dangerous. But only if all thirteen skulls are found. Until then we are safe. I'll be speaking about this potential future threat in confidence with the Aryan elders in days to come as they have some information on the subject. Right now, we deserve a chance to unwind and relax our minds. Let me propose a toast." Mitch said.

Mitch held up his glass and five more joined him."Long live Azorka." They shouted together.

The Wizard was lost in thought and staring at a bottle of his best rum. He had finished comforting Amy and she was resting. The Wizard's thoughts were revolving around his biological magic. He would make adjustments to a new formula and produce a race of super-smart creatures. The creatures would mature at the same rate as Azorka's Zapatsaurs and they would rely upon Amy for support and guidance. The crystal skulls full recovery will be an endeavor worth the effort. The future will be more predictable with the Wizard controlling the time lines. The world will be controlled by the Empire.

The Wizard walked over to the cabinet and poured himself a double rum. He walked to the large window behind his desk and drew back the dark gold curtains. Outside it was a bright sunny day. The Wizard held up his drink in a silent toast. He wasn't sad about his loss but optimistic about the future, although he still hadn't discovered the capture of the Dragon Queen.

"Long live the Empire." The Wizard shouted.

About the Author

I enjoyed a career in the Plastics Industry for twenty-two years, believing that I was saving trees, by producing vinyl siding for homes. During the time I worked for this large multi-national organization I was offered the opportunity to attend college, fully paid for by my employer. I successfully completed my courses in Marketing, Business Psychology, Sales, Management in Industry. Unfortunately, by 1995, the protective layers of our atmosphere were breaking down and plastic designed to weather and maintain its color outdoors was fading from more intense UV rays from the sun. Today our trees, the most precious resource on this planet, are facing extinction from climate change.

I developed more respect for our environmentalists fighting for change.

In 2017, I was concerned about the conflict between Russia and Ukraine. If we had a neutral committee organizing meetings and proposing solutions, perhaps the conflict would never have boiled over into the horrific consequences of war.

I believe that as a civilization, we need to have more respect for God, our planet and ourselves.

I hope to appeal to a younger generation, with my creation of two advanced societies fighting for dominance, in order to solve the problems of a world developing a lust and passion for war.